This is a work of fiction. All of the characters, organizations, and events portrayed in this novel are either products of the author's imagination or are used fictitiously.

A LOVELY DROP: A STORY OF THE NEVERNEATH

ISBN: 978-1-954998-06-3

www.DaryndaJones.com

Available in ebook and print editions

Created with Vellum

For Andrea

A LOVELY DROP

A STORY OF THE NEVERNEATH

DARYNDA JONES

CHAPTER 1

A uniformed police officer guided me from my seat inside the prisoner transport van to the open door, probably because my navigating the cramped interior while blindfolded and sporting a nifty set of cuffs was proving rather difficult. Odd, that.

He paused to tug the hood off my head. I squinted against the dull light of a misty gray morning, refusing to visualize my hair after such treatment. Denial was a wonderful coping mechanism.

The uniform nodded for me to continue, and I ducked under the opening only to stumble down a grated step. I didn't have ankle chains on or anything, but spending three days in a dingy interrogation room only to have a hood thrown over my head so I couldn't see where we were going as we weaved in and out of city traffic had disoriented me.

Thankfully, the uniform had a strong hold on my arm. He steadied me, but the second I had my footing, I jerked out of his grip. What can I say? I was irked. The authorities had never charged me with a crime, yet they held me for three days against my will. No phone call. No legal representation.

I had rights!

Or so I thought. Thanks to the Homeland Security Act and the fact that I had identified a known terrorist in my last attempt to help them solve a crime—this one a fatal bombing at Union Station in Chicago—they had all the authority they needed to hold me as long as their tighty-whities desired. The way I saw it, I was one step away from an extended stay at Gitmo.

The uniform gave me exactly three seconds to orient to my new surroundings before leading me through a smattering of cop cars. Their lights flashed silently against the brittle, leafless trees around us. We were definitely not in the city anymore. Probably an affluent suburb. I lived in a suburb, too, but this one smelled like young families with good jobs. Moms in the PTA. Kids in lacrosse. My suburb was a little less…family friendly.

The cop lifted a strip of yellow crime-scene tape, signaling with another nod for me to duck underneath before leading me past several other officers. They stood in a huddle in front of a small house, the kind with a white picket fence and rows of colorful flowers lining its borders. Only it was winter, and what was left of the flowers lay dead under a crunchy layer of fresh snow. The cops stared at me as they spoke softly to one another, their breaths misting in the crisp air. A heaviness blanketed the area, one that had nothing to do with the gray morning.

Something happened here.

Something bad.

When I realized what was going on, my lungs seized in surprise, and I almost stumbled again. This was a test. They wanted to see what I could do. To see if I was lying or, more likely, to see if I was in league with a terrorist organization. I should have known better than to send a note to Chicago PD telling them who'd planted that bomb.

Like always, I'd sent it anonymously, but of course they would bend over backwards on such a heinous and high-profile case. I'd been so careful. No fingerprints on the paper. A generic printer. Envelopes available at any office supply store. I'd used no local colloquialisms. Left no DNA as I hadn't licked the envelope to close it. I even used cash when buying the ink cartridge at OfficeMax. What gave me away? Where did I screw up? How did they find me?

However they did it, they'd probably ransacked my entire apartment looking for evidence, but by that point I'd been handcuffed and carted away as fast as their spit-shines could carry me. I asked for representation, but when Homeland got involved, lawyering-up was not always an option. The disappearance of three days of my life was proof of that.

At first, I'd refused to talk. Who would believe me, after all? But after thirty-three and a half hours of the same questions over and over with absolutely no cooperation from yours truly, they threw me in a cell and, it seemed, completely forgot about me.

On the third day—or possibly night—they dragged me out to begin the questions anew. Another six hours and I broke. Kind of. I disguised the truth in a sea of bullshit, as though I were only kidding when I told them I could go to a spot, any spot, and drop back in time up to 24 hours. I could see what happened at that spot prior to—and during—a crime, but someone behind the observation mirror called a stop to our little party the moment those words left my mouth. As though he knew. As though he believed me no matter how insane the idea. The interrogation ended immediately and thirty minutes later, I was cuffed, hooded, and tossed—literally—into a transport van.

A deep voice caught my attention as we crunched up the snow-covered sidewalk. My focus shifted from the red door beautifully decorated with a fall wreath to a group of men on my left. One of them was the voice behind the mirror. Even through the intercom it'd had the same smooth tenor. The same hint of impatience sprinkled with a healthy dose of anger.

I studied the group. The angry one, the impatient one from the observation room, caught my eye. While most of the men on scene were uniformed officers and wrinkle-suited detectives, the man with the issues was dressed more…clandestinely.

He had straight, shoulder-length black hair that matched the long duster he wore to a T. It was an odd accessory for an area filled with parkas and trench coats. His hair was in bad need of a trim, as was the shadow along his jaw. It framed a sculpted mouth that lured my gaze as he spoke, his deep voice soft but no less impatient, no less bitter than before.

A set of perfectly white teeth flashed occasionally as words fell from his mouth in irritation, and I stared long enough to get the whole group's attention before practically stumbling up the steps of the house. Right before I lost sight of him, his hard gaze met mine. Clear blue eyes shimmered like the ocean on a summer's day. They were shadowed by impossibly long lashes, the anger sparkling between those lashes unmistakable.

No, not anger. Contempt?

I turned away, my brows furrowing in concern as I stepped into the house. An assembly of officers looked toward me, each holding a cup of piping hot coffee. The aroma made my mouth water as the officer led me through the melee to the kitchen where a man summoned me with a quick wave of a gloved hand, a man I assumed to be the lead detective. He was also one of my interrogators. I'd studied each of their faces when they questioned me. Vowed never to forget a single one.

Only two detectives stood in the kitchen: the lead detective in his late forties and an attractive female, late thirties, dark hair pulled back into a loose chignon. She wore a scarf with pumpkins on it draped around her neck. Her expression was one of curiosity, not the antagonistic mistrust that lined her partner's face. I liked her and wondered how much harder she'd had to fight to get such a coveted position with Chicago PD.

A smattering of small easels with numbers on them sat about the room marking points of interest, and the unmistakable red patterns of spattered blood colored the walls, white cabinets, and stainless gas stove. An island blocked my view of the floor to where most of the blood spatters led, but I would've bet my lily white there was a large pool of the stuff behind it.

My stomach lurched and I swallowed hard. Blood and I didn't exactly get along. When I'd first decided to try using my ability to solve crimes, the violence astonished me. And the blood gushing from bodies like a floodtide made my head spin, making every 'drop,' as I called them, a little harder than the previous.

My gaze landed on a pumpkin sitting atop the kitchen counter. A small one meant for decoration. It wore a bright red smile, the shade a perfect match for the blood on the counter next to it. Apparently, whoever did this was an artist.

No matter, I thought as I drew in a deep breath. I was better.

"You're not going to hurl, are you?" the male detective asked, easing away from me. Murphy. I thought his name was Murphy.

I offered him my best glare.

He smirked. "So," he said, pointing toward the blood-soaked kitchen, "what we have here is a murder-suicide." He demonstrated by drawing a circle in the air around the main concentration of blood, as though anyone could mistake it for something other than the aftermath of a very violent event. His dark gray eyes locked with mine. "What do you think?"

I blinked in surprise. Why would they bring me here? This was some kind of test, yes, but why? They couldn't have possibly believed what I'd said. I'd buried the truth in a sea of ridiculous lies. Surely, they didn't believe me.

Even if they did, I had two choices: I could refuse to help, thereby proving I was involved with the bombing, or I could help and give them access to a new and improved secret weapon. Did I dare submit, prove my innocence, and lose my soul in the process? Or did I resist and possibly condemn myself to a life behind bars?

I welded my teeth together and set my jaw. Even if they did believe me, no way was I dropping in front of them like a circus freak. I would not be belittled or heckled or teased. I'd seen what they did to my mother. I'd seen how they treated her, used her repeatedly until she crawled inside a bottle and drown in it.

Seeing the damage they'd done had destroyed me as a child, and I swore I'd never be used like that by anyone for any reason. She'd lived through hundreds of horrible crimes as they happened, and I watched helplessly, unable to fully understand what she was going through.

Knowing what I know now, I would've crawled inside a bottle as well. By the time it was all said and done, by the time they'd broken her and kicked her to the curb, a notorious section of organized crime had picked her up, dusted her off, and used her even more until there was nothing left but a shell of the woman I once loved more than air. And these people expected me to follow the same path. Not in this lifetime.

"You said it yourself," Murphy added. He had a shaved head and a stocky frame that reminded me of a boxer from a cartoon. And he drank too much in his off hours if the red-rimmed eyes and swollen features were any indication. His drinking was either because of or the cause of his impending divorce. A pale line where a wedding ring once sat circled his finger. "You said you could *see* things." He added air quotes for effect, because his abrasive use of the word "see" wasn't transparent enough.

I pushed back a lock of my ridiculously unruly hair. *Vibrant,* my mother had called it. *Decadent.* I called it a pain in the ass. I would have killed for straight brown hair growing up. Or black. Or blond. Anything besides the recalcitrant crimson mop that sat atop my head like a spoiled princess.

The female detective watched my every move with purpose. Studying. Assessing. While Murphy watched my every move with something other than the most noble of intentions. There was both hunger and disgust when he leaned in to me, which did not speak well of his marriage. I wasn't psychic or anything, just a wicked-good observer.

And I had trust issues.

"Well?" he questioned with a raised brow. "You gonna show us your dog and pony?"

"Back off," a male voice said from behind me.

We all turned as the man in the duster walked in followed by the older gentleman he'd been conversing with on the lawn, the one who looked like he ate nails for breakfast.

"We'll take it from here," he said.

Murphy shrugged, clearly not giving a fuck. "As you wish, *Special Agent Strand.*" He backed away and swept his arm in a gallant gesture of surrender. Then he smirked again, waiting for the show to begin.

Good luck with that.

The duster, or *Special Agent Strand* of probably some obscure branch of Homeland Security nobody'd ever heard of, ignored him and turned toward me, stepping so close I had to crane my neck to look up at him. His sculpted mouth, the most revealing of all tells, remained impassive, making him unreadable. He took his time absorbing my features while his gave nothing away. After a long and quite unnerving stare-down, he began.

"September 2016. Two murders in the girls' dormitory at Purdue. No suspects."

My attention snapped into place so fast, it cracked audibly in my ears.

"August 2017," he continued. "Elderly man run down in Chicago with his grandson. No suspects."

My gaze didn't stray a hairsbreadth from the cerulean depths of his. The world around us faded away.

"November 2017. Seven-year-old girl vanishes from an elementary school in Wheaton. No suspects."

I didn't blink.

"February 2018. Woman found beaten and barely alive, dumped outside of a Des Moines emergency room. No suspects."

I didn't breathe.

"March 2018. Teller killed in a bank robbery in Grand Rapids. December 2018. Arsonist sets fire to half of Milwaukee. March 2019. Con man steals the life savings of every single resident at the Sunny Hills Retirement Home in Indianapolis." He stepped closer, staring down at me until we were practically nose-to-nose. "Those and a dozen others. All with no suspects."

I stood in shock that someone had put it together so thoroughly. My mind raced for an answer of how. What had I done wrong?

"Shall I continue?" he asked, his voice as smooth as bourbon.

I swallowed audibly but stood my ground.

He offered me a quick nod of acknowledgment, as though

accepting my silence as his cue to continue. "All of those crimes had no suspects. Zero. Yet all were solved through a series of tips from either anonymously-delivered phone calls or letters that contained names, addresses, and even drawings of the person or persons the informant IDed as the perps. All the letters were dropped at the corresponding police stations by a woman who kept her face hidden from the cameras. Not a single clear shot of her in the bunch."

His face softened as his gaze slid to a lock of hair that had stubbornly refused to stay put behind my ear. "But in one, the woman was delivering a letter during a storm and one lock of curly red hair fell out from under her cap."

My lids drifted shut in disbelief. One lock of my ridiculous hair gave me away. Then again, how much could they get off of one lock of hair? I lifted my lashes and stood in silence, afraid to say anything that might incriminate me.

"No comment?"

After a long moment in which my fight or flight response warred with the logistics of the situation—How far could I get, really?—I forced myself to calm and think about this rationally. I didn't do anything illegal. What could they charge me with? Aiding and abetting an investigation?

Collaboration. Of course. There were sicko serial killers who collaborated all the time. Terrorists were notorious for having an entire cell of like-minded individuals.

I lifted my chin with a new determination. "I asked for a lawyer three days ago."

"I asked for a pony when I was seven. Clearly, we've both been disappointed. What do you need to make this work?"

The change in direction threw me a moment. He wasn't kidding. He actually expected me to do this right here and right now. I'd never dropped with an audience in my life, and I damned sure wasn't about to start now. That was one thing my mother taught me: Never let them see your secrets.

"I have no idea what you're talking about."

"Save it," he said impatiently, turning from me at last.

Relieved, I filled my lungs to the brim. His gaze was as intense as a cobra's.

"Clear the room." He waved everyone but the nail eater out.

"Seriously?" Murphy said as his partner hooked an arm in his and practically dragged him from the room.

After the two detectives and the officer who'd escorted me in left, the older gentleman nodded, giving the agent the okay to continue.

He crossed to the island and leaned back against it to look at me. "We've been watching you for some time now, Ms. Grace. Or can I call you Andrea?"

"You can call me a cab."

"We know that you go to a crime scene and somehow figure out who committed the crime. Your tips have led to the arrest and eventual conviction of ninety-eight percent of the perps you've IDed. Ninety-eight percent. That's unheard of, and that's just what we know about." He sharpened his gaze as he tried to figure me out. "I want to know how you're doing it."

"Ancient Chinese secret. And besides, Murphy—" I pointed to the door the detective just left through. "—said this was a murder-suicide. You've clearly already solved the crime. Why do you need my input?"

"Humor me."

I crossed my arms over my chest. "I'd rather not."

He glanced down at his feet, his brows knitting in thought, and said slowly, methodically, "Perhaps I need to make something clear to you."

My throat tightened at the tone of his voice. It wasn't angry or bitter at the moment. It was…resigned. As though he had a job to do, and come hell or high water, that job was getting done.

"Right now, you're facing charges of terrorism and collaboration in every single crime you've helped solve. The way I see it, you're looking at about 500 years. Give or take. You have absolutely no rights and," he said, pausing for effect, "if I may say so, your ass is mine to do with as I will. Unless you prove to me otherwise, I'm going to have to assume you belong to a terrorist organization."

"You know that's not true. If you've linked me to all these other cases, why—"

"You're focusing on the wrong aspect here."

I bit down, feeling as though my life—my freedom—was slowly slipping through my fingers. "Which aspect should I be focusing on, then?"

One corner of his mouth lifted into a humorless smile. "Your ass."

"My as—?"

"And the fact that it's mine."

I took a long moment to answer, the concept so implausible. "I have no choice."

"Now you're getting it," he said with a wink that was the opposite of flirtatious.

I couldn't believe this was really happening. My mother had warned me. "Never try to help them," she'd said. "They'll squeeze every ounce of life out of you. They'll rip out your insides for the sheer pleasure of it then toss you away like you're nothing. Never try to help them."

At the time, she meant people in general. The gift ran in my family, passed down from mother to daughter for hundreds of years, though it did tend to skip several generations at a time. And throughout our history, my ancestors had learned not to help people. They'd only come back for more. It would never end, and they would resort to blackmailing us to keep our secret—our gift—from becoming public knowledge. Then everyone would want a piece, and there were only a limited number of pieces in every soul.

I listened to my mother. I heeded her warnings. I kept my head down. Got good grades. Graduated and got a decent job. Trusted no one. Then she died. She died and half of me died with her.

I crawled inside of myself and stayed there for months. A darkness had settled over me and I'd felt my soul withering away. It wasn't until I accidentally stumbled upon a crime scene after going out for milk that I began to resurface. I stopped at a small house in my neighborhood covered in yellow crime-scene tape. I stepped closer, curious, puzzled, and before I knew what was happening, I'd allowed myself to drop.

I heard my mother's words as time rewound before me. I heard her telling me to stop. To keep walking and don't look back. But I was so curious. I wanted to know what all the flashing lights had been about the night before. What brought about such commotion.

Then I came to the moment the woman was attacked. The violence ripped me out of the drop before I'd meant to leave it, but I couldn't go back in. I didn't dare. With bile burning the back of my throat, I dropped the milk and ran home, and that time I didn't look back.

But I couldn't get the memory out of my head. The man's face haunted me for days. The pleasure he took from what he did to her. The enjoyment. I finally sat down and drew the man's face the best I could, all those years of art classes paying off as I stuffed my hair into a Cubs baseball cap and delivered it to the police station in an envelope with the chief's name scribbled on it.

And suddenly everything was better. I'd done my duty. I'd assisted in a murder case. I'd been traumatized by the violence, sure, and it still woke me on occasion, but I'd done the right thing, and I felt the sun on my face for the first time in months.

And now this. After years of assisting the police, *this.* This...angry, bitter man. A man who was trying to make me do something I swore I never would.

He pushed off the island and stepped closer once again. With the stance of a fighter, he eyed me from underneath his thick, dark lashes. Waiting. Seeming to relish the idea of me refusing.

"Just you," I whispered at last, barely able to believe I was actually negotiating, the idea of me dropping with an audience impossible to comprehend. "No one else."

The older man spoke up. "I think that's my cue."

Agent Strand nodded without taking his eyes off me and the man turned and walked out.

"Remember what we talked about," the man said over his shoulder before the swinging door closed behind him.

The special agent didn't answer. He didn't blink. He was too busy staring me down, and I was back to avoiding his gaze. But everywhere else I looked, blood.

"What do you need?" he asked, his voice not as harsh as before.

I shook my head, incredulous. I was actually going to do this. I was actually going to drop in front of another person.

Then I remembered, I did do it in front of someone once. A group of someones, actually. I'd done it at a birthday party when I was a kid. They laughed in surprise at what I'd told them—basically that Toby McClure's mother was flirting with the mailman—and I was suddenly the most popular girl there.

Sadly, my mother found out from Toby McClure's mother, a devout Christian according to rumor, who saw what I did as sacrilegious. She screamed in my mother's face and threw words at her like "devil worshiper" and "burn in hell." I wasn't allowed to go to another birthday party until I was in my teens. Until I was old enough to understand the ramifications of what I'd done.

I drew in a deep breath and glanced around. "I just need something to hold on to," I said, my voice thin. I often came out of a drop disoriented. I wasn't the most graceful being on the planet as it was. Add a spinning world, and I had a tendency to lose my balance. And take things with me. Breakable things. And I wasn't about to use the island to steady myself. There wasn't much blood on it, but there was enough to keep me at bay.

Sensing my thoughts, he looked around then walked into the next room and came back with a dining room chair. "How about this?"

"That'll work."

With a quick nod, he sat it on the floor with the back facing me.

I held out my hands, indicating the cuffs still around my wrists.

He reached into a pocket in his jeans, and I got a better look at his clothes. If I didn't know better, I would say he was part of a motorcycle club like the Hell's Angels. He wore a leather vest under the duster and a T-shirt under that along with jeans and heavy motorcycle boots.

Watching me like a hawk watches a mouse, he pulled out a key, stepped forward, and took hold of my wrists. He didn't unlock the cuffs immediately. Instead, he held my hands in one of his a long moment before pushing the metal up my forearm a bit and rubbing the bright pink line where the cuffs had sat. Long fingers tested the area, his hands strong and elegant at once. Lightly kissed by the sun. And warm. Much too warm.

When I tried to pull out of his grasp, he tightened his hold and slid the key into the lock. The moment the cold metal left my wrists, I felt a hundred pounds lighter.

I rubbed the sorest spots then looked back up. "Nothing's going to happen," I said, schooling him in my strange ways as he stepped back to the island. "You won't see anything out of the ordinary. No fireworks. No gusts of wind howling through the house. No fog gathering at my feet. From your vantage point, it will simply look like I closed my eyes a moment. I should know. I filmed myself dropping once. I was curious."

"How does it work?"

"Told you," I said, taking a calming breath. "That's a secret."

"Meaning you don't know."

I'd already closed my eyes, but I allowed a small smile to part my lips just as I felt the world drop away. "Exactly."

CHAPTER 2

Water. It felt like warm water rushing over me when I dropped. Sometimes it stole my breath as though I'd literally jumped into a warm swimming pool. The water rushed over my nerve endings, up and up until I was completely submerged, until I wasn't inside myself anymore. Until I was someone else.

At first, I saw only the residual light from the room creating shadows against the backdrops of my lids. Then I could see through them as though I'd slid out of my body and was somewhere else. Someone else. That was when I knew I'd descended.

I stepped back, out of myself, and rewound time, but only a few seconds. I'd been looking down when Agent Strand unlocked the cuffs from my wrists. This time I watched him. His face. His eyes. I watched the slight crease in his forehead as he looked at the marks the cuffs had made. I watched his expression when he pushed them up my wrists to reveal how chafed they had become. I watched his full mouth narrow as he ran his fingertips along a particularly deep groove where the cuffs had cut into my skin. I found his concern both fascinating and unnecessary. The deep grooves had happened while I was busy stumbling either down steps or up them.

I decided to check out one more thing before rewinding the day all the way. I went outside and reversed time to the point where I walked up with the cop. Agent Strand was talking to the nail eater, but the look he gave me as I passed spoke volumes. I wanted to know what he was saying.

"How do you think she's doing it?" the older man asked right after I'd almost stumbled up the steps.

"She told us," Agent Strand said.

"She was bullshitting. That's about as plausible as a lunar production of Ice Capades."

"I read her, Gill. She wasn't lying. In fact, it was the first time during the entire interrogation she was telling the truth."

How the hell did he know that? Was I really so transparent?

"You went to a lot of trouble to set this up," Gill said. "If for some crazy reason—one that will change my entire universe—she can do this, then what?"

"Briarwood."

Briarwood? Briarwood, Indiana? If so, it was a tiny village of only about 16 people south of La Porte. I knew about it because I had set a story there in middle school. I needed a really tiny town and that was the tiniest I could find near my hometown on Google Earth. Either way, my teacher was not impressed with my story.

"You want to use her for that?" Gill asked.

"I want to know how my best friend and the best agent you've ever had ended up dead along with Kerrigan and every single occupant of a town they weren't supposed to be in."

What? The entire town? They were all dead? How was

this not all over the news? Did it just happen or were they intentionally keeping it quiet?

"Okay. I'm going to let you run with this, but just don't be too disappointed when—"

"I know the drill," he said, heading inside.

Gill nodded and started to follow when he called out to him. "You're wrong about one thing, though."

Agent Strand turned to face him. "What's that?"

"He wasn't the best agent I've ever had." The older man's face softened as he took in the young agent.

Strand shook off his comment, stiffening his shoulders as he continued inside.

I walked back into the house, preparing mentally for what I was about to witness. I stepped past cops frozen in time and studied the owners of the house through their décor, the way they arranged their furniture, the colors they used. They were young, vibrant, and well organized. Although everything grayed and became slightly transparent when I dropped, giving the area a hazy, ghost-like appearance, I could tell they used lots of fall colors, and I wondered if they changed the décor with the seasons.

Stepping through a uniformed cop, I made my way to a side table where the couple had let a week's worth of mail pile up. The envelope on top had both their names on it: Rob and Veronica Padgett. Pictures on the walls and scattered about the living room would put them in their early 30s. They had fresh faces, Veronica's much darker than her husband's, and bright smiles.

I glanced toward their bedroom through the transparent cops and transparent walls. I once wondered why everything was transparent when I dropped and came to the conclusion that I was not in any sort of reality. I was literally seeing ghosts of the past, even the ghosts of objects as it were.

I was transparent as well. I could see the tile floor through my hands. It totally freaked me out the first time I'd dropped, but I was only seven when it happened and my mother—hoping the gift would skip my generation—had yet to tell me anything about the big family secret. She'd told me there was one, of course, but I'd always thought it was the fact that my uncle was a perv. Dropping, a spiritual form of time travel, had not been on my radar.

The bed in the bedroom was made. There was a shirt and a pair of pants thrown over the back of a chair. Otherwise, everything was in its place. The Padgetts were neat, their lives orderly, and judging from the warmth of the décor, the care taken in both choice and placement of each item, they were happy. Then again, this could be one of those Sleeping with the Enemy situations. Rob could have been abusive and controlling. One simply never knew what went on behind closed doors.

No more stalling. Because that's what I was doing at that point: Stalling. Without any further ado, I closed my eyes—though I could see through my lids regardless—and dropped. Time reversed around me. People rushed past my periphery. The clock on the mantel spun backwards. Fresh flowers on the side table folded into themselves to sleep once again.

I turned away from the kitchen and hurried time along. I wanted to go back to the beginning without getting a sense of what happened there. I wanted to start the day anew, to see what the Padgetts had done that morning. Had they fought? Argued at lunch? I dropped as far as I possibly could: 24 hours from my starting point, before I felt the resistance that always let me know when I got close to my boundary.

It was an energy pushing me back, only letting me go so far, like a mother in a mall, pulling her child away from the escalators. I could have gone farther. I could see time falling away like the steps on the escalator, disappearing into the great unknown below, but because of that tug, because of that invisible gravitational force, I could only go so far, I could only get so close, before very bad things started to happen.

When I emerged from the drop, the clocks were 23 hours and 57 minutes from the moment I dropped. I'd checked my watch. 7:12. Now, the clocks read 7:15.

I heard a woman's lyrical voice coming from behind me. "You're going to be late." I turned to see Veronica making coffee.

Rob walked in, fidgeting with his tie. "Do I really have to wear this?" he asked before offering his wife a soft peck on the cheek.

"Your mother is paying you a surprise visit this morning, and she loves that tie."

He took a huge bite of a bagel then mumbled through his full mouth. "If it's so hush-hush, how is it you know about it?"

Veronica crinkled her nose. "I think she suspects."

Rob glanced at her in surprise. After a moment, he walked up, wrapped an arm around her waist from behind, and let his hand flatten against her stomach. "Did you spill the beans?"

"No, I quit my day job," she said with a chuckle. She poured coffee into a travel mug, secured the lid, then handed it to him. "Not a word. You have to promise."

"I promise, but my mother is like a bloodhound. She knows when I'm hiding something. Always has."

Veronica placed both hands on her belly, and I realized she must be pregnant. If she was, she wasn't far along.

After Rob went to work, I fast forwarded through Veronica's day. She cleaned the kitchen, did some laundry, watched a couple of soaps, took a long bath, and read a book on what to expect during the first trimester. Just as she was about to start dinner, Rob called to tell her his mother was having a dinner party and insisted they go.

"Did you tell her?" she asked, crestfallen.

"I didn't say a word. She guessed." I could hear his voice over the phone, the adoration he felt for his wife coming through loud and clear.

"Fine, but I'm not naming the baby, yet, no matter what your mother says."

"Deal."

Veronica put the food back in the fridge then sat at her dressing table to sweep her dark hair into a beautiful twist. Then she spent the next thirty minutes trying to decide which dress to wear when her phone rang again.

She answered it, waited, then said, "Look, I'm having this call traced as we speak. The cops will be at your house any minute. I'd run." A second later, she held out the phone to frown at it. "That's what I thought."

Rob walked through the door and she ran to meet him. Grabbing his hand with a giggle, she led him to the bathroom. "Your shower is ready."

"Are you implying I smell?"

"We are going to be late," she said, chastising him with the arch of her brows as she tugged off his tie.

"I had a client."

"You always have a client," she said as she headed for their closet. "Red or blue?"

"He was more of a pasty white."

"Your tie. Red or blue."

"Purple."

She leaned into the bathroom. "Your mother hates purple." She thought a moment, then said, "Purple it is."

He stripped and slipped into the shower. "I need help with something."

She rolled her eyes. "No."

"Please. It's going to be really embarrassing if we don't take care of this before we get to my mother's house."

Veronica laughed as she strode back to the shower, screamed as he pulled her in with him. "I did my hair," she called out in protest.

"I like it better down anyway."

They had fun, flirty sex, while I stayed in the kitchen and fast-forwarded. Then they left the house in a flurry of coats and scarves. I was beginning to wonder where the unhappy couple was that dies in a murder-suicide not two hours from now. Unless they got into a terrible argument at that party, they seemed like the happiest married people I'd ever seen. Nothing out of the ordinary happened all day. Well, besides the phone call.

I fast-forwarded to get to the nitty-gritty of the evening, but a sound, like a drum roll, caused me to slow time back down. I rewound then listened again. A slow, methodical thud was coming from somewhere behind me.

I turned to see a kid in the living room, and the creep factor skyrocketed. Where had he come from? What was he doing in the Padgett's house?

I watched him as he stood at the front window, eyeing the driveway as though waiting for the couple to get home. And he never stopped hitting his head against the wall. The rhythm never changed. His focus never strayed. Finally, his head started bleeding.

I stepped over and studied his features so I could draw him later. His thin mouth was drawn into a severe line, his fists clenched at his sides, his brows drawn hard over his dark eyes. He was young, probably still in high school or recently graduated. He had muddy brown hair, a threadbare jacket, and baggy jeans. And his features weren't quite right. They were disproportionate from each other, as though he'd been born with a mild case of fetal alcohol spectrum disorder, if there was such a thing as a mild case of FASD.

I continued to watch as thin rivulets of blood dripped down his face, yet he never stopped banging his forehead against the wall. Never wavered from his vigil, not until we saw headlights pull into the driveway. A clock on the mantel struck midnight just as the couple walked in through the back door. The kid moved at last, walking silently into the dark hallway that led to the bedroom.

"We're going to miss it," the husband said as they stumbled into the kitchen. He turned on a television on the island and surfed the guide until he found what he was looking for.

I wanted to scream. I wanted to warm them, to tell them there was someone in the house, but the deed was already done. I was literally watching ghosts, like a horror movie on replay. There was nothing I could do. I couldn't touch them. I couldn't change what happened. I could only watch helplessly as the atrocities that kid was capable of played out before my eyes.

His wife laughed softly as she put a plastic container in the fridge. "Oh, my god, what is this supposed to be exactly?"

"Hell if I know," he said, settling onto a stool at the island. "Some kind of meat. I was afraid to touch it. We might need to rethink these dinners, hon."

"Agreed," she said with a smile in her voice. She paused and looked over her shoulder. "Turkey or ham?" She was going to make a sandwich to make up for the horrendous food they were served at the dinner party.

A voice echoed throughout the room as a talk show host named Max Midnight performed his opening monologue. "And what's with the president's drinking problem?"

The audience burst into a chorus of well-timed laughter

as Max continued ragging on the president's most recent faux pas at a state dinner.

"Ham," he said, absorbed in the monologue. "No, turkey. No, ham."

She chuckled and stepped next to him to catch a bit of the show. "You know, this might sound crazy, but I think you can have both."

His head snapped toward her in feigned surprise. "Are you sure? I won't get arrested?"

"Well, I wouldn't announce it to the world or anything, but your secret will be safe with me."

With a huge smile crinkling the edges of his eyes, he wrapped an arm around her before grabbing the remote to turn up the volume. "There it is!" he said, his excitement infectious.

I stepped around to see what all the fuss was about. "Here at Padgett and Cline, your family comes first."

It was him, Mr. Padgett, and he was in a commercial for a local insurance company. He must've owned it with a partner, and they'd done a commercial. That was what all the excitement was about. And here I thought he just really liked late-night talk shows.

His wife clasped her hands over her heart. "You look amazing," she said, truly enjoying her husband's fifteen minutes.

"It's all the makeup. I'm thinking about using it every day now, or no one will recognize me from the commercial."

She giggled as he squeezed her waist. "A little foundation will do wonders. I have one that makes you look ten years younger."

Ignoring the rest of the commercial, he looked over at her, appreciation glittering under his lashes. "Are you saying I look old?"

She grinned and smoothed a lock of hair at his temple. A graying lock of hair. “Not at all.”

He started for her neck with a growl when he stopped and looked toward the back hall. “What’s that sound?”

I’d been lost in their happiness, drowning in their bliss when the thudding sound hit me again. My heart stopped beating as both his wife and I followed his gaze. The kid was still in the dark hallway, banging his head against the wall again.

It was almost time.

I braced myself and, as selfish as it sounded, I hoped this wouldn’t take long. Would he torment them? Torture them? Or would he make it quick?

Mr. Padgett stood to investigate, but the kid slid along the wall and showed himself in the doorway. Before anyone could react, he raised a gun. My hands flew to my mouth when he fired. Mr. Padgett lunged to protect his wife, taking a bullet in the chest. He gasped for air, his face the picture of shock as the kid fired again. My hands curled into fists. Bile rose to the back of my throat as I watched another bullet strike Mr. Padgett’s midsection. Then his shoulder.

My mind registered a high-pitched scream.

Mr. Padgett looked back. “Run, Veronica,” he said before collapsing onto the island and sliding to the floor in front of her.

In this strange world of transparency, I watched as Veronica ducked behind the island and draped her body over her husband’s, her shoulders convulsing with sobs.

The kid walked around the island and watched her cry. Her body shook uncontrollably as she looked up at him. Her stunned expression proved she knew exactly who he was.

“Travis?” she asked, her voice paper thin and raw with emotion.

Without uttering a word, he lifted the gun and fired again.

My lungs seized as her head jerked back. She seemed to hover there, as though time had stopped for her as well, before she fell forward and collapsed onto her husband.

I dropped to my knees, fighting the sobs clawing at my throat.

The kid tilted his head to one side as he examined his handy work. The blood splatter on the cabinets seemed to fascinate him. He stepped over the lifeless couple, dipped a finger into a small pool that had gathered on the countertop, and drew a smile on a decorative pumpkin before walking out the back door without a care in the world.

I should have followed him. He could have dumped the gun nearby. I could only go so far, about a hundred feet in any direction, but I could have watched him just in case. Did he have a car? A motorcycle? A bike? Anything that could help the authorities identify the killer, but I couldn't do it. I had to get out. I had to go back before I got lost. It had happened before and the outcome had not been good.

With one last glance at the Padgetts, I released my hold on time and skyrocketed back to the present. The moment I felt my physical body again, I crumbled to the ground beside the chair, catching my weight with the palms of my hands and dry heaving onto the tiled floor.

Agent Strand would be confused. When I dropped at a point in time, I returned to that exact point. To him, it would appear as though I bowed my head, paused a second, then fell to the ground gasping for air. He would think my reaction an act. A performance.

Then again, screw him.

I steadied my breath and looked up. He stared down at me, doubt lining his face, before stepping forward as though to yank me to my feet. When I jerked out of his reach, his anger multiplied. I could see it in the constricted lines of his face when I looked up.

He did this. He sent me in there believing I would witness a murder-suicide. He knew that wasn't what happened. He'd lied to me. They had all lied to me. Especially Detective Murphy.

CHAPTER 3

Before the agent realized what I was doing, I scrambled to my feet and ran for the hall that led to the dining room. Bursting through the door, I spotted my target: Murphy.

I rushed toward him and started swinging the moment he was within arm's reach. My fist made contact. I had to see a brutal murder and they seemed to think it was a joke. I was a joke. Like it wouldn't affect me.

Still, I was attacking a detective in a room full of detectives and uniformed officers. They would have to arrest me, now. It was the law. But at least I would be incarcerated for something I actually did. And they would have to process me. I would finally get my phone call. I could get a lawyer and do something productive about my situation.

Agent Strand pulled me off Murphy. It was probably for the best. The detective had reddened with rage and he was approximately one nanosecond away from planting my face into a wall. That would have sucked, but he'd lied to me.

I fought the agent to get back to Murphy. I kicked and swung, clamoring to scratch out his eyes even though blaming him for this atrocity was like blaming our soldiers for the Vietnam conflict. It wasn't Murphy's fault. I knew that. I did. Somewhere deep down inside. But my anger at his lying and the cost it had on me, what I was forced to witness, just grew stronger with each beat of my heart.

Even though the truth wouldn't have changed anything. Even though I never knew what I was in for when I dropped. This time I had thought—had hoped—to be more prepared. I expected a heart-wrenching tragedy. I expected violence. I knew it would not be easy no matter what had happened, but still I'd been prepared for one thing and got another. I clawed at Agent Strand's arms, tried to squirm out of his grip for another go at the arrogant detective.

"Calm down!" Strand said into my ear, his voice harsh, but I couldn't. The unfairness, the needless violence, the senselessness had hijacked all my faculties.

I used to watch movies with gratuitous violence without giving them a second thought. I hadn't been able to watch one since my first drop at a crime scene. My whole life changed. I no longer saw violence as entertainment but as a reality, and I had to trim as much of it out of my life as I could. And then this. This day. This tragedy.

Agent Strand finally got his arm around me and pressed me into the wall as a couple of the other detectives in the front room held Murphy back. I was lucky they were there.

"What the fuck?" Murphy yelled at me as he tried to push past the barrier. "What the hell did I do?"

"You lied to me!" I screamed over Agent Strand's shoulder. He held me pressed against the wall, his body like a bank vault door. I ground out the next words, my revulsion with Murphy clear. "You said it was a murder-suicide. You lied."

Agent Strand looked down at me, the blue of his irises sparkling with surprise as he studied me. I watched him with breath held until I felt his hold loosen.

With a mental shake, I pushed out of his grip, but I didn't dive for the detective again. Red meant stop, and Murphy's bald head was glowing scarlet. But just to be safe, Agent Strand placed a hand on my shoulder, letting me know he was still there as Gill, the older man he'd come with, walked innocuously past the panting Murphy to come face-to-face with yours truly.

"Ms. Grace, I'm Deputy Secretary Terrance Gill." He held out his hand—*now he introduces himself*—and I looked at it bewildered. What was the deputy secretary, a man I assumed was pretty high up in the grand scheme of things at Homeland Security, doing at a crime scene in a suburb of Chicago?

When I didn't take his hand, he continued unfazed. "What do you mean Detective Murphy lied?"

I glanced at the offending detective before elaborating. He glared back, brushing spilled coffee off his jacket and huffing with unspent anger. "He told me this was a murder-suicide. It was not."

The deputy secretary eyed his colleague.

Agent Strand didn't move.

"Can you elaborate?" the man asked me as he took my arm gently and led me back into the kitchen. A place I most definitely did not want to be.

When I hesitated, Agent Strand was at my back, urging me forward.

We entered the kitchen followed by several of the other investigators, suddenly eager to hear what I had to say. I'd never done this. I'd never divulged what I could do to the common, as my mother had called them. Those who were not like us, like the women in my family, were common.

Before we could get into it, I had to ask a question. I glanced at the island, knowing the crime scene had been processed and that the couple had probably been carted off hours ago, but I still had to ask. "Are they still there?"

"Who?" Agent Strand asked.

I looked over my shoulder to glower at him. "The Padgetts. The people who died last night. Who else are we talking about?"

He glanced back at Murphy. "How much did you tell her?"

"I didn't tell her anything," he said, his voice full of skepticism. "But their names are on the mail in the entryway. It's not rocket science."

Ah, yes. Another thing I learned early on. The common can explain away anything. Absolutely anything. A UFO could land in their swimming pool and they'd have an alternate explanation all ready to go.

Murphy's partner placed a reassuring hand on my arm. "No, honey," she said, her voice reassuring. "They've been taken to the morgue. Take your time."

I nodded, grateful for the camaraderie, and continued. "Well, unlike what some people might want you to believe, the Padgetts did not die in a murder-suicide scenario. A kid named Travis killed them."

The room erupted in quiet conversation. The deputy secretary shushed them with a glare. "Can you explain?"

After drawing in a deep breath, I ran them through the whole scenario, from the Padgetts going out to eat, to the kid banging his head on the wall by the front window, waiting for them to come home. From the commercial on the television to the kid aiming a pistol at them, a stubby one with a round cylinder that only holds six rounds. I told them how Mr. Padgett tried to protect his wife. How she wouldn't leave her husband when he told her to run. How she uttered the boy's name, Travis, right before he shot her in the head.

By the time I was finished, my cheeks were soaked with tears. I didn't wipe them away. I wouldn't give them the satisfaction of knowing how much it killed me to not only watch what happened to the Padgetts, but to have to relive it as well.

"I can draw him for you if you'd like. The kid."

Murphy's partner handed me a tissue, and I finally got a chance to see her badge up close. Detective Anne Marie Williams. I turned away from everyone to use the tissue, but I turned right into Agent Strand's chest. He stayed his ground, letting me use him to block out the rest of the room.

"There's no blood in here," Murphy said, his skepticism at an all-time high. He'd walked into the living room and was examining the wall.

I swiped at the tears with the tissue and walked to the doorway. The kid must have cleaned it up while I was watching the Padgetts.

"Test it," I told Anne Marie. I walked forward to point it out. "It should be concentrated here with streaks of his blood here."

Without another question, she did. She grabbed a kit, sprayed the area with a chemical, probably Luminol, then shined a black light on it. Residual blood glowed a purplish hue and Murphy almost gasped aloud.

"How can you know that?" he asked, but Strand had questions of his own.

"Can you describe this kid?"

I did, giving as much detail as I could. "About my height, messy dark hair, a long nose, and a wide mouth. He had thick eyebrows and wore an old dark blue hoodie with a dolphin logo on the left shoulder. I really can draw him if you need me to. It doesn't take long."

They sat me at the dining room table with a piece of notebook paper and a pencil. Strand sat across from me as the rest of the team examined the scene for more clues to Travis's identity, using the information I'd given them.

"You don't know why this kid did it?" Strand asked me.

"No. He never said anything. Not a single word. He just banged his head against the wall and pulled the trigger. Oh!" I said, almost shouting. "He drew the smiley face on the pumpkin. You should be able to get his fingerprint off it."

Strand stifled a sad smile. "We already did. There were no matches, which simply means he's never been arrested."

"Really?" I asked, as I added a shadow along the kid's long nose.

"That surprises you?"

"Well, yeah, kind of. I mean, he raised that gun and pulled the trigger like it was nothing. Like he'd done it a thousand times." I lowered my head as a fresh round of tears threatened to push past my lashes. "He didn't hesitate." My voice cracked, so I stopped talking and just drew. Strand let me gather myself before starting the questions anew.

"How can you do that?" He pointed to the drawing.

"Oh, part of the gift, I guess. I have a photographic memory."

"She was a high school teacher," he said. "Mrs. Padgett."

I raised my head in surprise. "Maybe Travis was one of her students."

Anne Marie walked in to glimpse my drawing. "Yep," she said, "I'd say he was." She held out a book, a yearbook from the year before. "Travis McCall. Is this your guy?"

When I looked at the picture, my stomach tightened. I bent slightly with the threat of heaving. All I could see were his cold, dark eyes as he lifted the gun. The void of emotion in them as he shot and killed two innocent people as though he were simply taking out the trash. "Yes," I said, trying not to hyperventilate. "That's him."

"Good job," she said. "We should be able to get his fingerprints or a DNA sample for comparison without too much fuss considering the severity of the crime."

"She was pregnant," I added, and my audience stilled,

including Murphy who was pretending to look for evidence a few feet away from us. "Mrs. Padgett. They didn't want anyone to know yet. I got the feeling she was having trouble carrying to term, so the minute she found out she was pregnant, her husband insisted she leave her job."

Anne Marie turned to her partner.

Murphy nodded. "Padgett's mother just confirmed."

"That's right," I said, remembering. "He had lunch with his mother yesterday. He said she suspected. I think that's why they went to dinner last night. To celebrate."

Murphy nodded again.

Anne Marie leaned in to me. "You may have just solved a double homicide, honey."

She was so nice and trying to be so positive, but all I could think about was how the room was spinning and nauseating. I thanked her then rose to get some air. Strand followed me.

Neither of us could miss the sideways glances Murphy kept sending my way, and I wondered if Strand went with me to protect me against the burly man or to make sure I didn't decide to pull a Houdini.

Once outside, I filled my lungs with crisp autumn air, savoring the scents of fall as a school bus rumbled past us. Tiny faces peered from the windows behind shadowy reflections of fall leaves. Some of the children wore soft, dreamlike smiles, unaware of the horror that lay mere yards away.

After a moment, my surroundings quit spinning long enough for me to say to Strand, who was pretending not to watch me, "We better hurry."

He'd raised a brow in question.

"Briarwood."

He stilled and his expression morphed into something I had yet to see from him: Absolute astonishment. "How do you know about Briarwood?"

"I listened in on the conversation you were having with your boss when I first walked up before dropping back to the crime. Your partner? Your best friend? He died there along with everyone else in Briarwood. I can only drop back twenty-four hours and the case here has already been solved. We're wasting time."

It took him a long moment to say anything, but when he did, it wasn't to me. He took out his phone, punched a couple of buttons, then lifted it to his ear. "Power up. We'll be there in five."

A HELICOPTER. I was in a helicopter. And I did not like it. Not one bit.

We landed 45 minutes after we took off and I had no idea what to expect. Seconds before we touched down, Strand leaned toward me and secured a huge gas mask onto my face. It made me very uncomfortable for several reasons. First, it looked like an alien had attached itself to my face and was trying to impregnate me. Second, Strand wasn't wearing one but everyone else was, so I'd clearly taken his. And third, the eerie stillness of the tiny town crept up on me the moment we landed.

We sat down in a school parking lot, and there was no traffic, no pedestrians, no store owners or mail carriers. In fact, there was no movement at all. In the distance sat a line of cop cars with lights flashing. They were blocking the road going into town. The area had been quarantined.

"This is stupid," I said to Strand, the mask muffling my voice. He needed a mask just as much as I did.

He furrowed his brows in question as he lifted me out of the chopper. His hands, warm against the icy wind caused by the roaring blades above us, spanned the circumference of my ribs. "What?" he asked, yelling over the thunderous sound.

Before I could answer, he wrapped an arm around me and ushered me away from the chopper. The deputy secretary followed and we were met by a team of investigators in white containment suits. Wonderful. All I had was a facemask and Agent Awesome—a man apparently impervious to the effects of lethal toxins—stood completely unprotected.

Once the chopper lifted off, I straightened and tried to do something with my hair. It was poking out from beneath the straps of my facemask in every direction imaginable, but my mortification subsided when I looked past the hazmat team to the entrance to the school. There on the sidewalk lay a neat row of body bags and the world fell out from under my feet.

CHAPTER 4

"Andrea?"

My lids fluttered open to the sound of my name on a deep, smooth voice. I brought Strand's face into focus. A lock of dark hair fell over his eyes as he watched me. He ran his fingers through it with one hand and held out a glass of water with the other.

"That was quite a spill," he said, his expression full of concern.

I wasn't sure how to feel. People didn't concern themselves with me. It just didn't happen. "Sorry. I've seen a lot of death in the last few hours."

Hours. I blinked past the fog. Hours. We were running out of time! I bound off the cot, wondering in the back of my mind where we were.

"Whoa," Strand said, catching me to him with one arm. He placed the glass on a desk behind him then put his hands on my shoulders. "Take it easy."

"How long have I been out? Where are we? How much time do we have?" It was odd. All the things I could do with time, yet there never seemed to be enough of it.

"You've only been out about twenty minutes." He ducked to look into my eyes as though making sure I was coherent.

Trapped in his blue gaze, I stated the obvious. I was good at that. "We're not wearing masks."

Something terribly sexy tugged at one corner of his mouth. "They've tested the area. It's clean, but we have no idea what it was. We're hoping you can rectify that."

"I'll do my best."

After another second or two of that penetrating gaze, he snapped to attention and sat back, dropping his hands. "I guess we should get to it, then."

I nodded and he led me out from behind a stack of metal boxes where they'd tucked the cot. The tent was packed full of equipment, much of it like something from a science lab. People came and went in a rush. Each seemed to have a job to do. A helicopter roared overhead as though searching the area.

"What exactly am I looking for?" I asked as a kid brought us both bottled water. An absolute bundle of nerves, he dropped Agent Strand's twice before achieving a successful handoff.

"What's with him?" I asked when we exited the tent.

Strand had been watching me. He always seemed to be watching me, and I wasn't sure if it was because he was still trying to figure me out or because he thought I would bolt. Where would I go, for goodness sake?

"Who?" he asked.

I almost laughed. He had to notice the kid's behavior. I raised my water. "The kid who brought us the water."

"Oh, that. Yeah, it's a groupie thing. I have somewhat of a reputation in the department." His chest swelled comically. "I get a lot of admirers."

Trying my hardest to stifle a laugh, I pointed to a gathering in the distance. "What's going on there?"

Strand sobered. "That's where my partner died. They think he may have been trying to stop this from happening, so they're canvassing the area. I thought we could start there."

Suddenly worried there would be a body there, I slowed.

"They moved all the bodies while you were out. It's okay." He put a hand on the small of my back, encouraging me to keep walking.

We trekked up a hill to where the group was gathered. The deputy secretary stood off to one side. He walked over to us, his features more haggard than they were earlier.

"Can you do it again?" he asked me.

"Whenever I want."

"Then let me reframe my question. Do you want to do it again?"

I let a sad smile slide across my face. "Never. But I'll do what I can."

"Can I watch this time?"

"There's not much to see," Strand said. "It's instantaneous."

"From your point-of-view," I corrected. "From mine, it can seem like hours or even days before I jump back. I can turn back time again and again. But, yes, you can watch."

He nodded and stepped to the side to let us work.

I scanned the area. There was nothing around us, really. We stood in an empty field behind the school, and the school was one of only five or six buildings in the entire town. They had a post office, a small store, a tiny gas station that looked like it had been closed for several decades, and a couple of churches. "I'll drop and see what I can see, but I can only go so far."

"Twenty-four hours," he said.

"No. Well, yes, but I mean distance-wise. I can only go about one hundred feet in any direction, then I have to switch locations. I'll look under every rock, though. If there is an answer to be found, I'll find it."

Strand nodded, seeming grateful. "You might listen in to Mark's conversation. He died here with another agent, Ed Kerrigan. I want to know what they were talking about."

"You got it. Mark was your partner?"

"Has been for years. We were working the same case but from different angles. And then this."

"Can you give me more?" I asked. "Every little bit helps. What exactly are you working on?"

"I could tell you," he said, then stopped, allowing me to finish the statement in my mind.

"Gotcha. Pictures?"

"Mark Cham was undercover. All pictures of him are classified."

"That doesn't help me much."

"Trust me. The minute you see Mark in action, you'll know it's him." He glanced around. "I'm not sure what you can hold on to out here." He shrugged then held out his hands. "Me, I guess. If I'll work."

Surprised, I hesitated before placing my hands in his. When I did, his swallowed mine in both size and warmth.

"You ready?" he asked, squeezing my hands lightly.

I braced my feet slightly apart, took a deep breath, then nodded. The moment I closed my eyes, I dropped.

I scrolled back the entire 24 hours then slowly made my way forward in time. It didn't take long for something to catch my attention. I stopped and watched as a man of Middle Eastern descent ran across the field we'd just walked through. He tripped but got back up again, turning full circle, searching the area. He seemed frazzled and afraid.

"Over here," another man said, emerging from the trees in a gully below us.

I walked closer to get a better look.

The Middle Eastern man hurried to him. He wore an orange coat and ill-fitting jeans. Dark wisps of hair curled out from underneath a baseball cap. Add to that a full beard and it was hard to make out his features. The other man was about Strand's age with a sport coat and tie, which was odd considering the trek it took to get here. His shoes were polished with bits of wet grass on them, and his hair was cut military short. This had to be Mark.

"You have to hurry," the Middle Eastern man said, pushing an envelope into Mark's hands, his eyes saucerlike.

"Adiv," Mark said, taking the envelope with a casual ease that was the exact opposite of Adiv's hurried demeanor. "We have time. You said it yourself. Your boss isn't even in the country yet."

"No." He seemed to calm a bit. "No, you are right, of course. Please, forgive me."

"There's nothing to forgive," Mark assured him. He opened the envelope and read the contents. "This is perfect. We have the location and the time. We'll be there."

"You better be or I'm dead. If he thinks I betrayed him—"

"He won't," Mark said.

I hurried over and glanced at the paper before he folded it and put it in an inside pocket. It had the name of a café in Gary, Indiana, but I still didn't know what the sting was all about. According to Strand, Mark wasn't even supposed to be in the area. He also said that two agents were killed here. I glanced around for the second agent. Nothing.

Adiv couldn't help himself. He scanned the area, too, for good measure, his gaze darting from one object to the next like a frightened rabbit. Seeming satisfied, he turned back to Mark. "Do you know who the inside man is, yet? My boss is nervous about doing business with an organization that allows undercover agents to penetrate it."

Mark gritted his teeth. "No, damn it, but I will. I have a guy on it."

"If this man has infiltrated your organization, why don't you already know who he is? He has to be new, right? You can't tell a fed from a biker?"

"I have a guy on it," Mark said, growing frustrated with the man. "We're watching two possibilities."

"You have *two* narcs?"

"No." He raked a hand through his hair. "Two possibilities. We're checking them out. Doing deep background checks."

"Why? Just kill them both. Be done with it."

"It's not that easy. We'll catch the leak. Look, asshole, this is shit you wouldn't understand. Your boss is the one who decided to do business with a motorcycle club. Don't get me wrong, it's the club's interest I represent, but they're about as trustworthy as my ex-wife."

"I'm beginning to understand that. My boss was in prison with the leader or something. He trusts him. You're the one he doesn't trust. You'll be at the exchange?"

Mark steadied his gaze. "Sure. As long as your boss has the money and this information is correct. You're absolutely certain it's correct?"

"Yes, I'm certain." Adiv turned again, looking like he was about two seconds from bolting. As he turned that time, however, Mark reached behind his back. But before I could blink, Adiv had drawn and leveled his gun on him, his aim steady, his frightened demeanor gone. In its place stood a man of calculating stealth like I'd never seen before.

Mark stopped and put up his hands. "Easy there, Adiv."

"On the ground," Adiv said, motioning for Mark to get on his stomach.

"Put the gun down, son," Mark said.

Adiv was not impressed. "If I have to say it twice, your sex life ends right here and now."

I couldn't help but notice Adiv's Middle Eastern accent had disappeared.

Mark acquiesced, crawling onto his stomach then placing his hands on his head. "Your boss will hear about this."

"My boss, fuckhead, is Deputy Secretary Terrance Gill, and you have been a very naughty boy, Ed."

Ed? Who was Ed?

The guy who was apparently not Mark gaped at Adiv, but only for a minute. Without warning, he rolled over and went for his gun.

Adiv was right on him, gun in his face. Even I wouldn't miss at that distance, and I was a horrible shot.

"Really?" Adiv asked, incredulous. "Take it out, Ed. Two fingers. And I still hold the record for marksmanship at Langley, so don't even think about it."

"Who are you?" Ed asked, taking the gun out of his pants with his index finger and thumb. He tossed it at Adiv's feet.

I remembered. Strand had mentioned another agent, Ed Kerrigan. So then who was Adiv?

Adiv kicked it away. "What happened to you, Ed? Working for a motorcycle club as their lawyer was supposed to be a cover. When did they turn you?"

"About ten minutes after I fucked your wife up the ass."

He seemed bitter.

"Yeah, well," Adiv said as he pulled out his phone, and began dialing. "What can I say? She likes anal. Special Agent Mark Cham. I need a—"

He stopped, his brows furrowing as he scanned the ground a few feet from him. Then he seemed to get woozy. He looked back at Ed and I followed his gaze. Ed's mouth gaped open like a fish fighting for air, his eyes wide, frightened. Not two seconds later, he stopped. Just stopped. He lay unmoving. Completely lifeless.

I turned back to Adiv. No, Mark. This was Strand's partner. Special Agent Mark Cham. He dropped his hands and both the phone and the gun slipped from his fingers. He stood motionless for several seconds, as though he'd died even before gravity took hold. The next moment, he crumpled onto the wet grass beside Ed.

My hands flew to my mouth. It was so sudden. So fast. So surreal.

At least I could tell Strand his partner didn't suffer. He was so brave, in fact. So dynamic. I could see why the two of them were close.

Sadly, the bit about his partner was the only thing I could tell Strand. I didn't know anything they didn't. Or I thought not.

Farther up the mountainside that surrounded the small town sat a pickup. I found it odd because of the way it was parked, looking out over the town. Looking out over Strand's late partner. It stayed there a few minutes as I tried to run up the mountainside toward it, but the trek was harder and the truck farther than either looked. With a newfound determination, I released time and reemerged in front of Strand.

"Hurry!" I shouted, running back to the town.

"What?" Strand asked, following me.

"We have to hurry. I'm almost at the edge of my twenty-four hours. We have to get up there—" I pointed to the lookout. "—fast."

"Wait." He pulled me to a stop. "Wait, what happened?"

"Strand, we don't have time. Can you order him?" I asked Deputy Secretary Gill as he hurried behind us. "I'll explain everything, but first I have to get up there." I pointed again in case they missed it the first time.

"Go," the man said.

For a split second, I thought Strand was going to argue. Instead, he took my hand and ran with me over the hill to a parked police cruiser. "We need to borrow this," he said to the cop standing beside it. Before the guy could respond, we were in his vehicle, turning the engine over.

"Are we going to wait for your boss?" I asked as Gill ran toward us, but the deputy secretary waved us on.

Strand peeled out, took a couple of turns and sped up the mountainside. I wanted as much time with this person as possible, to learn as much as I could before the minutes crept up and pushed me out.

The moment Strand put the car in park, I lowered my head and dropped, flying into the past as far as I could.

I looked down at the field we'd just come from. The man pulled up beside me in a white pickup and parked as Mark ran across the field. Just as before, he stumbled, scrambled to his feet, and kept running. Knowing what I now knew, I lauded his performance. Strand's partner had fooled me completely.

I turned and focused on the man in the truck. Walking through it, I took in as much as I could. The interior was splotched with dirt-covered oily patches, most likely the work truck of a mechanic. A sloppy mechanic. With thick, wavy hair, olive skin, and clothes that looked casual and yet tailor-made, the driver didn't look like a mechanic. Then again, Strand's partner didn't look like a special agent for Homeland Security. Still, if nothing else gave him away, his watch would. It was far more expensive than anything a mechanic would wear.

An envelope on the dashboard was addressed to a Beau Richter, but the discarded soda cups and sandwich wrappers, mostly from McDonald's and the like, told me this guy was probably not Beau Richter. He was lean and healthy, and I doubted that he would ever throw a soda cup onto the floorboard of anything he drove.

The truck was clearly stolen. The only thing that might have been his was a duffle bag on the seat beside him. It looked brand new, like he bought it just for this occasion.

He took a cell phone from his pocket and dialed a number, but he didn't put the phone to his ear. Instead, he set the phone on his thigh, reached over and pulled a gas mask out of the duffle bag.

It was him. He'd killed everyone in the village, including two agents with Homeland Security. Was he deliberately trying to throw the agency off his tracks? Or was he just killing an agent who got too close and took a whole town with him? That seemed a bit extreme even for an extremist.

None of this was making sense. The driver pulled the gas mask over his head then checked his watch. Keeping his arm on the steering wheel, he looked out over the field and waited for his victims to succumb to whatever he'd just sent out. The detonator must have been triggered with the phone call.

I strained to scan the area, searching for where the chemical weapon could be. I ran to the front of the pickup, my torso swimming through the engine, and emerged on the cliff of the steep drop in front of us.

I couldn't stray too far from my body. I'd learned that a long time ago. But I needed to find that weapon. Unfortunately, I had no idea what I was looking for. It could be no bigger than my pinky, for all I knew. I should have asked Strand for more information. I should have asked him what to look for.

The next time I scanned the area, both men below me were dead, and I still had no weapon. The driver sat a few moments more, then started the engine and drove up the mountain. I wondered if he was going higher to escape the gas. Maybe it was a dense gas and would linger closer to the earth. Maybe he would go up there to wait until it dispersed and he could leave the area safely. Or, more likely, the road led over the mountain and continued on the other side.

I contemplated his escape route a few seconds more before turning back to the field. My heart went out to Strand's partner. I would help catch his killer any way I could. For him and for Agent Strand. Not that he'd done me any favors, but this wasn't about favors. This was about a mass murderer, including the unforgivable act of killing children.

I'd never tried to scale down a mountain in a drop before, but that was exactly what I was going to do. Every time I released time to change position, I lost precious minutes. I didn't want to lose a single second, so I sat down and stepped out over the side, surprised there was no guardrail. Anyone could drive off this thing.

The thought terrified me, and even though I could hardly be hurt by falling down the side of the mountain in my incorporeal state, the thought of trying to scale down it terrified me as well. I drew in a deep breath, metaphorically, and slid over the side.

The act proved much easier than it would have had I been flesh and blood. I eased down the side and climbed to my feet, brushing my hands together to wipe off nonexistent dirt. Then I searched. It had to be around here somewhere. It had to be close if Mark was the original target. I rewound time again and again as I looked under every nook and cranny. I worked for what would have been hours had I been in real time and I got absolutely nowhere.

Just when I was about to give up, I remembered something. Running back to the scene where Agents Cham and Kerrigan fell to their deaths, I rewound again to just before they passed out. Special Agent Mark Cham was holding

Agent Ed Kerrigan at gunpoint, but he looked down. At first, I thought it was because he had inhaled the poisonous gas and grew confused, but as I watched him, I realized he had turned to a sound. There was a slight click then a soft hiss nearby.

I followed Agent Cham's gaze and sure enough, about three feet from where Kerrigan lay was a grouping of tall grasses. Because it was transparent to me, I could see a small silver needle poking out of the ground underneath it. And underneath that was a much larger cylinder full of the deadly gas that had been released into the atmosphere. I'd found it.

Elated, I looked back just as Agent Cham collapsed. I stood horrified with myself. No, I didn't find it. Agent Cham did. It was just too late for him, but at least I could help catch his killer.

With a newfound determination, I released time.

Sadly, time did not release me.

This had happened once before. I'd strayed too far from my body despite the tug of an invisible tether that kept me anchored, and I'd stayed away too long. The longer I stayed, the more transparent my surroundings grew. Eventually, they would disappear altogether and I would be lost again. I would be alone in this great emptiness and I would grow a little more insane with each passing hour as time spiraled out of my control. I could no longer get a hold on it. Instead, it passed through me like a rush of icy wind. Eons came and went, and I could swear I felt the creation of the universe at one point.

Fear tightened around my heart. I had no idea how long I'd been away, but I did know that if I could just find my body, I could force myself back into it. Last time I got lost, it took me what amounted to weeks to find myself again. I had to catch a glimpse of myself in time. It wasn't like finding a needle in a haystack. It was like finding a particular needle in a mountain of needles.

The glimpse I found was of my body in a hospital in a coma. It was the one and only time I'd entered my body at a different point from when I'd left it. And it was not an experience I cared to repeat.

I fast-forwarded as I ran to the spot where Strand and I had parked. The world had dimmed so much more than I'd thought. It was almost completely translucent. How had I let time slip by me so carelessly? I scrambled up the mountain, but it disappeared. I felt myself falling through empty space just as it reappeared beneath me.

With every ounce of strength I had, I grabbed for the mountain and began to scale it again. Sobs of relief tore at my throat. The closer I got to my physical being, the stronger I became. I fought the effects of a celestial gravity, clawing at anything of sustenance I could find.

After an eternity, I made it to the top. I looked back. Emergency workers were barely visible in the mist of eternity. Did I miss it? For all I knew, days had passed. What would Strand think when I didn't come back? What would happen to me? Would I be in a coma? My mother had never told me about that part. Maybe she'd never experienced it. Or her mother before her.

These same questions had replayed in my mind over and over the last time I got lost as well. I had to get a grip. I had to stop and concentrate on finding the exact spot in time where I'd dropped.

The fall colors of the mountainside dissolved. It was almost completely white when a car appeared. A police cruiser. I almost dropped to my knees in relief. Strand sped around the last curve with me in the passenger's seat. I consciously released time again. When I opened my eyes, I was sitting in the police cruiser just as Strand was turning off the motor.

I covered my face with my hands, relief flooding every molecule in my body.

"Okay," Strand said. "Are you ready to do it again?"

I gaped at him with tears suddenly pushing past my lashes, realizing he had no idea I'd already dropped.

"Andrea?" he said, leaning closer.

Without another thought, I threw my arms around him and clutched his wide shoulders like my life depended on it. Deep sobs shuddered through me as I curled my fingers into his duster. He pulled me over the console and held me, and I couldn't have been more grateful if he'd saved me from a burning building. As far as I was concerned, he had.

He didn't ask any questions. For a few minutes, he just let my tears soak into his jacket, then I shot up, remembering why we were there and what we had to do. For a moment, his beauty stunned me. I gazed at him through what I could only imagine were puffy, redlined eyes.

His blue ones were full of concern. His full mouth formed a straight line as he tried to dissect my emotions. One brow formed a curious line as he gazed at me. He was breathtakingly handsome. I'd noticed before. It was impossible not to, but he seemed even more so now. For one thing, he was putting up with my sudden, colossal mood swing. He had no idea what I'd just gone through, but he trusted that I had a legitimate reason for my outburst. Nobody had ever given me the benefit of the doubt before. This was new. Refreshing. Ingratiating.

"Just don't pass out again," he said, a mischievous twinkle beneath his lashes. "'Bout killed me to have to carry you all the way to home base."

I gasped audibly.

"Damned near broke my back." That adorable tug

appeared again. It mesmerized me. His whole mouth mesmerized me. His whole face. What had I gotten myself into?

"I'm so sorry," I said, trying to squirm off him.

He kept his hold firm. "What happened?"

My perch was so comfortable, so…desired, it was hard for me to insist, but insist I did. I pushed away from him, suddenly embarrassed.

"I saw who did it and I found where he planted the weapon." Ignoring the surprised expression on his face, I continued. "The truck he was in belonged to a Beau Richter, but I'm fairly certain it was stolen. I did get a good look at the guy, though. Rich. Well-funded. I need paper and a pencil." I kept talking as I surveyed the area for something to draw on. "The chemical bomb, if you call them that, is under a grouping of tall grass about three feet from where your partner was standing. He was so brave, Agent Strand." I paused to tell him that. "Your partner. He was so brave and so skilled. And that other agent was dirty, but you probably already know that." I went back to looking for a pencil and paper. "Only the tip is sticking out of the ground."

"The tip?" His throat had tightened at the mention of his partner.

I paused again to make sure he was okay. "The bomb," I said. "The chemical thingy. Only the tip is sticking out of the ground. It's almost impossible to see."

He nodded, recovering quickly.

"This will work." I pulled a menu for an Italian restaurant in La Porte out of a side pocket. It had just enough white space on one corner for me to draw. "He used his phone to detonate it. You can check for tower pings, yes? Pencil. Pencil. Ah!" I found a pen in the cop's glove box. "He used a smartphone, but I doubt they have an app for bomb detonation."

I began to draw the man's profile, since that's what I saw the most of, when Strand put his fingers beneath my chin, turned my face toward his, and brushed a thumb across my cheek, wiping off an errant tear.

Once again, I was struck.

Before he could say anything, I pulled away from him and started to draw again. "You have to stop doing that."

"Doing what?" he asked, giving me the space and time I needed. His freaking voice was almost as bad as his freaking face. It was deep and smooth and sensual and made my insides tighten every time he spoke. Then again, I did have adrenaline avalanching through my veins at the speed of light. Maybe now was not the best time to fall in love with a guy just for being hot. Those relationships never ended well.

"Looking at me. Making me look at you."

I added a shadow to the bad guy's eyes then drew his nose. It was well proportioned. Long but thick enough so it didn't appear too long.

"You don't like looking at me?"

He was appeasing me, letting me do my work, giving me time to recuperate. "Please," I said as I turned the menu over and started on the frontal of the bad guy's face. I didn't get as clear a picture, but it was burned into my memory none-theless.

I should also draw his watch. I got the feeling it was custom made. Too much gold for my taste, and very out of place with the casual clothes he wore, but he was probably trying to fit in with the locals. He should have ditched the watch if he wanted to do that.

"Please?" Strand asked as I worked.

"Like any female on earth would not want to look at you."

"Is that a compliment?" he asked.

I blinked up at him, surprised. "No. It's just...I don't know. It's just a fact."

He nodded and let me go back to work. "Are you going to tell me what happened?"

"Mmm-hmm," I said, adding some finishing touches to my crude line drawing. It was about as good as it was going to get without an actual pencil and a clean sheet of paper. I handed them over to Strand. "So, this is the guy in the stolen truck who detonated the bomb. But he went up the mountain. Does this road go down the other side? I never saw him come back down. What about cameras in town? Did they have any? And what about the phone call to detonate the bomb? Can you get something off that?"

Strand hadn't looked at the drawing yet. After a long moment, he dropped his gaze to my rudimentary artwork.

"I'll do a better one. This is just for now."

"No need," he said, his voice soft with astonishment. "I know exactly who this is. And he's supposed to be dead." He cursed under his breath and turned away in thought. "I knew that intel was bad. Slippery fucker. If this really is Yousefi, if he really is alive, then he has something much bigger planned."

"Bigger?" I asked. "Bigger than killing everyone in town?"

"It's a small town. He's more of a blow-up-the-world kind of guy."

Dread flooded my lungs and tightened around my heart. "Do you think he has another bomb?"

"I think he's in the market, and I know exactly who's selling it to him."

"Who?" I asked, alarmed.

He bit down, lowered his head, and said softly, "Me."

CHAPTER 5

After the longest day of my entire existence, we pulled up in a black Dodge pickup to a hotel that had cabins for rent instead of rooms. I had to sign about a thousand documents before they'd let me go with Strand to help with the investigation, but by that point, I was in too deep not to help. Despite my mother's voice screaming in my head not to help them—never to help them—this was bigger than anything I'd ever been a part of. Hundreds, if not thousands, of lives were at stake. It was simply something I could not ignore.

The deputy secretary flew us via a private jet close to Waukegan, Illinois, where we found Strand's pickup waiting. We climbed inside and headed to the cabin he'd been living in for the past few months.

All I knew about our location was that we were close to Grayslake near an exchange point where they—aka, the bad guys—were supposed to meet the buyer—aka, Agent Strand. Apparently, he'd been undercover with a motorcycle club, trying to determine their connection with a terrorist organization and ultimately where the buy would take place.

Yousefi had shipped a chemical bomb as far as Mexico, and the motorcycle club had arranged for it to be smuggled into the country where Yousefi would then pick it up again. For a large sum of cash, of course.

Strand was not happy about the arrangements. He didn't want me around, and he'd argued with the deputy secretary. I was right there with him. At first.

When Gill took me aside and asked if I could assist them further, part of me felt like I was in it this far, I couldn't stop now. But another part of me wondered what on earth I could do. I dropped back in time. Big whoop. How was that going to benefit them in the long run?

Still, when Deputy Secretary Gill told Strand his plan and Strand had argued, the elation I'd felt at helping them this far deflated. I couldn't hear what they were saying, and normally I might drop to listen in on their heated exchange, but after my latest experience, I felt it pertinent that I not drop for a while.

And, as much as I hated to admit it, I was hurt by Strand's vehement refusal to take me with him. Hadn't I proven myself?

We didn't say two words to each other on the short flight or the drive to the cabin. He suddenly looked tired and I could sense the pressure he was under every time he worked that strong jaw of his.

He unlocked the hotel room, strode inside, and removed the duster. For the first time that day, I saw him. Every inch of him, albeit clothed inches. The impossibly wide shoulders. The tapered stomach. The trim hips and steely ass.

My god, that ass.

I couldn't tear my gaze away as he first checked the room, glanced out the window into the endless black night, then began to strip the nonessentials from his body. First the gun belt. Another gun hidden in a boot. A couple of knives pulled from clever places. Then his boots. I sank onto a chair in the corner, praying the pants were next.

"Do you want the first shower?"

I snapped to attention. "I…I don't have any soap. Or shampoo. Or clean clothes."

He nodded then turned on the bathroom light for me. "I have some soap and stuff. Probably not your brand, but they should get you through the night. And we've got clothes coming."

His jaw had grown more shadowed as the day wore on, framing his mouth to shapely perfection.

"Is that okay?" he asked, seeming annoyed.

I blinked, trying to stay focused. "That's fine. I'll go first. Wait. You have clothes coming?"

"Compliments of Gill. Our man should be here soon."

I couldn't imagine what they would come up with for me to wear. I wasn't the pickiest shopper, but I did have standards. With a wary nod, I rose and started for the bathroom.

He stopped me with another question. "Do you want to tell me what happened today?"

Did he mean when I burst into tears like a drunken drama queen at prom? No. No, I did not want to tell him what happened today.

"I'm okay. It was just a hard drop. It happens." As I strode toward the bathroom, he blocked the entrance with an arm.

"You're mad at me." It wasn't a question.

"No. I don't blame you for not wanting me to tag along. I get it. Boy, do I get it."

His scythe-shaped brows inched together. "Is that what you think?"

Afraid he would see the hurt in my expression, I turned away. "I'm okay, Agent Strand. Really. You may not have noticed, but I'm a big girl."

When he kept his arm there for an eternity and a day, I glanced up at him.

After a very long moment of contemplation, he said, "I noticed," then dropped his arm and went back to removing items from his person. "And call me Sebastian."

Sebastian. I liked it. And I liked his ass. I liked him, too, but that ass. They just didn't come any hotter. I didn't want to leave him. The pants had to come off eventually.

With the reluctance of a courtier going to the guillotine, I strolled into the bathroom and closed the door. The tiny room was outdated but clean. Couldn't ask for more than that after an exhausting day of tracking down bad guys. Very *bad* bad guys.

Having no other choice, I turned on the shower and stripped. It was no wonder Strand—Sebastian—was a tad on the touchy side. His best friend was dead. A despicable enemy was out there planning God only knew what. And he was here stuck with the likes of me. I felt bad for him.

Still, I had to wonder what the deputy secretary was thinking by sending me with his agent. I had no training. I had zero natural ability when it came to self-defense. And I knew nothing about terrorist cells beyond what I saw in movies.

Wondering what the man had up his sleeve, I stepped into the steaming shower and washed using Sebastian's soap and shampoo. I savored the scent of him on my skin. He didn't have conditioner, but the hotel had a tiny bottle. That would be enough for one washing.

No one understood the needs of corkscrew curls.

Before I turned off the shower, I heard a heated exchange of male voices. I shut off the water quickly and grabbed a towel. It sounded like two men arguing at first, Sebastian and someone else. But the more I listened, the more I realized it wasn't really an argument despite the fact that Sebastian was most definitely angry.

I stepped out of the shower and found fresh clothes awaiting me. They'd been placed on the closed toilet lid, and I gasped. Had he come into the bathroom while I showered? He had to have. The curtain was opaque, but still.

I used his toiletries to finish my routine the best I could, did a quick French braid to try to rein in the mop that sat atop my head, then pulled on the underwear, jeans, and sweater. All a perfect fit. Perhaps a little too perfect. I rarely wore my jeans so tight.

The sound of breaking glass startled me. I cracked open the door and peeked into the bedroom of the cabin. Sebastian was alone, his head bent, his hair hiding his features from me.

"What happened?" I asked him, peering around the room for bad guys. I'd had about enough of them, to be honest. Instead, I found a shattered goblet in the carpet and a wet spot on the wall, a telltale sign that the glass had been at least half full when it hit.

He turned as though he'd forgotten I was with him. "It's over. I missed the meeting."

Walking out barefoot, I stepped close, alarm rising in my chest. "I don't understand. The exchange? Yousefi has the bomb?"

He shook his head. "No. I was supposed to be at the exchange, but I missed the meeting the group had with him. Now I don't know where the exchange is taking place and Vince, the leader of the Disciples, feels that since I missed the meeting, I'm not fit to go the exchange."

"You have to try!" I said, putting a hand on his arm, pleading. "You have to find out where the exchange is, Sebastian. You have to go there and stop this."

Sporting a grateful smile, he turned to face me. "That was

never really the plan, love. I just had to find out where and when the exchange was supposed to take place. We can't risk losing the players or the delivery device by tailing them. There is an entire team waiting nearby, ready to setup at the exchange and be there when Vince shows up with the weapon and Yousefi with the money."

"So, you just need the time and location? That's it?"

"Yes."

I shrugged. "Why don't I just go in and get the information for you."

He turned away from me.

"Oh," I said, catching on at last. "That's why Gill wanted me to come. He knew you wouldn't make it back in time for the meeting."

"Gill can bite my ass," he said over his shoulder. "You're already in enough danger just by being here. Just by being with me." He stepped closer. Looked down at me. Wrapped a hand around my arm. "Vince's spy already spotted you. Now I have to give him the cockamamie story headquarters came up with of who you are and why I missed the meeting and say it in a way that won't get either of us killed."

"There's a story?" I asked, surprised. I looked down at the arm he'd grabbed hold of. His grip was firm but not painful in the least. "Shouldn't I be in on it?"

He tugged, pulling me closer. "That's why I didn't want you to come. You're not an agent, Andrea. You didn't ask for the dangers of this life. I signed up of my own free will, but Gill had no right to ask this of you."

I smiled. "I bet you were first in line, too."

"What?" he asked, confused.

"You said you signed up of your own free will. I bet you were first in line."

A frustrated grin lifted one corner of his full mouth. "How'd you know?"

"Gut feeling. But I can do this—"

"No," he said, dropping my arm. A chill swept underneath the sweater where his hand had been. "Not after today. Not after what you went through."

"That was entirely my fault," I said, embarrassed. "I… I almost got lost."

His brows furrowed, causing a slight crease between them. "I don't understand."

"In time. I almost got lost in time, but it was my fault. I strayed too far and stayed too long. I know not to do that."

He stared at me a long moment as though trying to understand what I meant. "The point is," he said, giving up, "all of that happened because you were doing the bidding of Homeland Security."

"How many children died?"

He stilled and leveled a deep blue gaze on me, his irises shimmering in the low light. "Seven."

I lifted my chin, trying to hold it steady. "And how many people are at risk?"

He lowered his head, his jaw working under the strain of his frustration. "Hundreds of thousands."

I stepped closer and glared up at him. "Don't ever ask me why I'm helping you again."

After another long moment of contemplation, he scooped up his duster. "Let's go, then."

"Wait," I said as he pulled me along behind him. "I need shoes."

"Oh, right."

"And so do you," I reminded him.

A quick glance at his own feet confirmed it. He raised a single brow. "I guess I do."

~

TWENTY MINUTES LATER, after a hefty trek through the woods, we slowed to a stop behind a group of bushes. A barn sat about twenty yards from us and through the slats we could see the glow of a fire inside.

"This is where they met earlier today," Sebastian said as I picked leaves out of my braid. "Are we close enough?"

I gaged the distance. "Yeah, this should be fine. I'll stay just long enough to get the info." When he offered me a worried expression, I said, "I've done this a thousand times, Strand. I just got carried away today. That doesn't normally happen."

"What can I do if it does?"

His concern was endearing. So was that severe line he'd drawn his mouth into. I had a hard time tearing my gaze off it, so I stopped trying. Just went with the flow and spoke directly to his mouth, hoping for that tug at the left corner again. "If I don't immediately open my eyes again, just put me on life support. I'll show up eventually, God willing."

No tug. My wit had apparently lost all its charm. It happened.

Before I could think it through, I lifted a hand and ran my fingertips along the outline of his mouth. He stilled and I glanced up—his eyes glistening in the soft glow that filtered to us from the fire—before closing my lids and dropping.

The first thing I did was freeze time to watch his reaction again when I placed my fingers on his mouth. It was so out of character for me. I was more of a duck-and-cover kind of girl.

Oh, I'd kissed guys before and I'd even had sex once, but at the ripe old age of twenty-four, I had yet to experience that extreme attraction that other girls felt the moment their eyes landed on a particularly scrumptious specimen of their liking. I chalked it up to trust issues. I also rarely squealed in delight or clapped my hands when handed a gift. I wasn't sure if that was a good thing or a bad one.

After watching Sebastian long enough to legally be considered a stalker, I rewound time until a group of men entered the barn. Three biker types. They'd ridden their Harleys up the dirt road and parked them along the side of the barn. I followed them in and watched as they built a fire. They were talking about this and that, mostly about a man they thought to be a snitch. Someone named Slider, and it occurred to me that I had no idea what name Sebastian went by while undercover. I prayed it wasn't Slider, because they had plans for that poor guy.

After a few minutes, Yousefi showed up and I had to force myself not to panic. The mere sight of him sent my heart into overdrive. He walked in with another guy, very small, very pale, very geek-ish. Yousefi's choice in companions surprised me before I realized a few minutes into their conversation he was the tech guy. He actually built the weapons Yousefi used to kill people.

Vince, a large man with broad shoulders, a broader stomach, and lots of graying facial hair shook his hand and offered their guests a seat around the fire. They'd set up folding chairs. Vince ordered one of his men to stand guard and the meeting commenced.

They talked about the good ol' days when Vince and Yousefi were in prison. They worked in the kitchen together and had formed a very unlikely friendship. A friendship that had Vince saving Yousefi's life, which would explain the trust. Vince jokingly asked Yousefi who'd pissed him off. Who the gift was for. It took me a moment to realize they'd been referring to the bomb as a gift the whole time. Yousefi laughed and said it was for the resident of a very large white house.

The White House? They were targeting the White House?

I almost stumbled trying to get back to my body, then I realized I still didn't know where the exchange would take place. Cursing to myself, I hurried back, rewound so I didn't miss a single word, and waited for them to decide on an exchange point and time.

More than anything else on earth, I wanted to hurry back and tell Sebastian, but these guys were nuts. They could come up with an idea only to change their minds a few minutes later, then where would we be?

So, I sat through another half hour of BS. Seriously, what on earth could these guys have in common? When the conversation turned to the technical aspects of the delivery device and how exactly they were going to get it close enough to the White House for it to serve its intended purpose—its main purpose being the demise of the President of the United States—it was so far over my head, my mind started to wander. Draping myself across a bale of hay in exasperation, I had to rewind three times just to get through it all.

At last, Vince and Yousefi stood. Vince walked him to the barn door, chatting the whole time before taking Yousefi's hand into his for a firm shake. Because they were partially transparent, I saw clearly the piece of paper that exchanged hands. Yousefi palmed the paper with a conspiratorial nod to Vince before heading out the door.

I bolted upright in a panic. What was on the paper? Was it a number in case of emergency? Was it a map? Was it a change of plans? I watched as Yousefi and his tech support walked up a path that led into the mountains in the exact opposite direction of where Sebastian and I waited crouched on the ground. I looked back, weighed my options, then realized I had to see what was on that paper before I lost him. I would never be able to find him again in these woods. I had to follow him as far as I could, now.

It had started to rain, hard, which explained why the forest was so wet around us on the hike up. The tech guy kept slipping, but Yousefi paid him no mind. They kept walking, growing more translucent with each passing moment. The forest around me dimmed, grew cloudier. Each step took me farther away from where my anchor, aka me, sat.

Finally, a parked car appeared before us. An older model Buick, so unlike the stolen truck he drove before. Yousefi got into the passenger side while his tech support ran around to the driver's. The moment the door closed, Yousefi opened the note at last. It was a picture of a marble statue, a Viking princess, if they had those, complete with a breastplate, long hair with tiny braids peppered throughout, two swords strapped onto her back, and wings behind those. She was beautiful.

Underneath the picture were the words Midday Eucharist.

I had no idea what it meant, but the moment the picture disappeared before my eyes, reappearing an instant later, I knew I'd pushed this drop as far as I dared. I filled my lungs —not that I actually breathed during a drop—and released time, praying time would release me.

A microsecond later, I was back with Sebastian. My fingers still lingering on his mouth. Surprise still evident in his smile.

I snapped my hand back. "We have to hurry!" I said, scrambling to my feet.

Sebastian grabbed me and threw me onto the ground. When I tried to argue, he covered my body with his and my mouth with his hand, his face mere centimeters from mine as he slid out a knife and nodded toward the barn. I glanced that way and realized two men were still at the barn. Or they'd come back. Either way.

One of them laughed out loud at something the other had

said. "Slider, where do you come up with that shit?" he asked him as they entered the barn.

My eyes rounded. I pried Sebastian's hand down and whispered, "That's Slider! They're going to kill him!"

He hissed in a breath then frowned into the night.

"They're going to kill him," I whispered again.

He closed his eyes.

"Sebastian, they think he's a snitch."

"He is a snitch," he said, regret hardening his features.

A floodtide of fear swept through me. "Is he your snitch, Sebastian? Does he know who you are?"

"No." He placed his forehead on mine, his warm breath fanning across my cheek and stirring a stray lock of hair. "Not really. He snitches to one of the other agents on-site, but he has no idea I'm one of them."

Relief washed over me until I realized that didn't change the fact that they were about to kill that man. "They're going to kill him," I repeated.

Sebastian sheathed the knife, rolled off me, then helped me into a squatting position. "There's nothing I can do without compromising our primary goal."

He was right. I knew he was right, but it didn't make it any easier. "Isn't there anything? Can't you call in your team or something?" When he didn't answer, I asked, "What if that were you? What would you do?"

The hard gaze he leveled on me knocked my breath away. "I'd die, just like he is about to. Too many lives are at stake, Andrea. We can't interfere." He started back down through the forest. "Did you get the information?"

We stayed low until well out of sight. My entire backside was soaking wet now and covered with mud. So much for the clean clothes. "I did, but there's a catch."

He paused and turned back to me. Even in the moonlight filtering through the trees I could see the deep blue sparkle of his eyes. My stomach flip-flopped and for the first time in a very long time, I wished I was pretty.

"What kind of catch?" he asked.

"I have to draw it."

"You have to draw the location?"

"That's not the catch. The catch is that there are two possible locations."

With a nod, he continued through the forest and I thanked God he had a good sense of direction. Photographic memory or not, we could have been headed to China for all I knew.

While I sat drawing the statue with one of those eraser-less short pencils and hotel stationary, Sebastian paced the room. He'd called Gill and told him about the meet they'd originally set up, then told him to hold for more intel. And that intel involved the speed and accuracy of both my memory and my artistic skill.

"So, he changed the plan?" he asked me for the tenth time as I drew the statue's lovely wings. "You're sure?"

"Yes. I'm certain of it, but I don't know why."

He nodded in understanding. "I do. That's the reason I was invited in the first place. Vince doesn't trust Corte or me. Well, he doesn't trust anyone, but he's having both of us watched."

"That explains why we had to crawl out the back window to get out of the cabin."

"Exactly. Even though Corte's been with him for years, this was a test. If feds show up at the exchange tomorrow, he's going to think Corte is either undercover or a snitch, and no amount of pleading will change his mind. Corte will die. Probably quite painfully." He looked down at me, his expression full of gratitude. "I would have died. I would've learned the mock location, and he would've known one of us was an agent. He would've killed both of us, just to be safe, and the feds would have come away with nothing to show for it. You've saved countless lives today, Andrea. Including mine."

A smile I couldn't have suppressed if my life had depended on it spread across my face. "All in a day's work, yes?"

"Sure. But now it's time for you to go home." He turned and started stuffing my old clothes into a duffle bag. My new clothes were still attached to my body, literally, wet and muddy as they were.

Disappointment bit hard into my stomach. For the first time in years—no, for the first time in my whole life—I felt like I was doing some good. Using my ability to really help people in a proactive way, not just after the fact. Not just after the murder or rape or robbery had occurred.

My mother had been wrong. I'd heeded her words so long that I'd become hollow inside. It was our duty, our responsibility, to use our gift to help others. With great power came great responsibility. I totally felt like Spiderman.

"But I'm not finished with the drawing," I argued.

"As soon as you are, I'll have a car come get you."

"What if something else happens and you need—"

"No," he said, turning back. "I won't put you at risk any longer."

"You dragged me into this!" I stood and faced him. Fury washed over me as I did. I poked his chest with an index finger to express it. "You did this. You . . . made . . . me . . . care. And now you're kicking me to the curb?" I set my jaw and rolled onto my toes to look him in the eye. I missed by a few inches, but I was at least a little closer. "I don't think so. I am in this to the end, and you can take your misguided and rather belated sense of honor and shove it up your ass."

He'd let me rant and rave for a few minutes. Afterward, I felt much better. And slightly vindicated.

"I'm going to finish this drawing," I continued, sitting at the table again. "And then I'm going to take a shower. I'm covered in mud, in case you haven't noticed."

I didn't look up when I heard him say softly, "I noticed."

CHAPTER 6

The day that I thought could not get any longer had indeed gotten longer. It was now midnight, and the exhaustion that should have overcame me was being held at bay by the adrenaline pumping through my veins. The exhilaration of finding out if anyone on Sebastian's team would know what this meant.

He was on the phone when I finished the drawing. I held it up to him and he stilled. After taking it from me, he told the person on the other end he'd call right back.

"This is what Vince handed Yousefi?"

I nodded. "She's marble."

"I've seen her. My father lives in Boston. This is from a church there."

A spark of excitement spiked inside me. "Do you know which one?"

"No, but I know it's on Clarendon."

I nodded and stepped closer to look at the picture with him. "And it explains the writing."

"It does?"

"Yes. Midday Eucharist, or a midday service where they do a holy communion. Wait," I said with a gasp. "You don't think they're going to release the chemicals in the church do you?"

"No. I think they are saving their big finish for the White House, like you said. The Secret Service has already been alerted, by the way. They'll be ready if we fail."

"I vote we don't fail. Just for good measure."

That tug reappeared at the corner of his mouth. "I'll second that. So, a midday service—"

"Three days," I said, interrupting. "They should only have a midday service this time of the year on a Sunday, right? And that's not for another three days, since it's officially Thursday." I tapped my naked wrist, suddenly wondering about my watch they never returned.

Sebastian checked his. At least he had one. "You're probably right."

"As per my usual state," I said, heading for the bathroom again. I was beginning to like that shower.

I stripped and washed all the mud off my body first, then went for the shampoo. I loved the woodsy scent of it, and the freshness of the soap he used. But I'd officially run out of conditioner. I peeked around the shower curtain just in case there was another bottle somewhere when Sebastian walked in, pretty as you please.

"Excuse me," I said, making certain he couldn't see anything pertinent.

But he was on the phone. He lifted a T-shirt and placed it on the closed toilet lid just like before. He'd stripped down to his own T-shirt and jeans again, both now covered in splotches of mud, and had ditched the duster, leather vest, and all the weaponry.

"Okay, hold on," he said, right before he put a hand over

the phone. "Did they mention anyone else while they were talking, anyone they might suspect of being a CI?"

"No," I answered, shrugging so he'd get the hint and leave. I was quite naked behind the curtain.

"What was Yousefi driving again?"

"An older model Buick." I thought back. "A blue LeSabre. Illinois license plate DDL-431. It had a broken taillight on the passenger side and a dent in the front fender."

He relayed that information, strolled out of the bathroom, then right as I turned off the water and reached for the towel, walked back in again. "License plate is registered to a college kid in Chicago. She drives a Chevy Cruise. The LeSabre was light blue?"

"Just blue." *Like your eyes,* I wanted to say, but didn't dare. "Normal blue with metallic."

He nodded and walked out again. I gave it a minute to make sure he didn't come back before grabbing the towel. I'd definitely have to braid my hair again, or walk around with a red powder puff on my head. My hair did not do well without product, and it was probably asking too much to hope Special Agent Strand would have a little hair gel on hand. I wondered if he always wore his hair that long or if he did it only for this gig.

I toweled off, raced to put on my bra, which was still mud-free, thankfully, and hurried to throw on the T-shirt he'd lent me for the evening. It fit me like an oversized dress, but it smelled like him. I gathered up a handful and buried my face, reveling in the scent.

He'd also left a clean pair of his boxer briefs, as my underwear was soaked. Thoughtful of him. They didn't exactly fit, but they were the stretchy kind and stayed in place for the most part. Then I threw on the clean socks he'd left and walked out to give him the room.

He was still on the phone, going over the plan for the next day. Someone would pick me up in five hours while it was still dark out, then Sebastian would head to Boston. He couldn't leave until Vince did or it would look suspicious, but they had men watching Vince's house and he was apparently packing to leave.

Still, they had to be careful. They didn't want to spook anyone by moving in too soon. Homeland Security had one shot at grabbing the device, and since no one but Vince knew where it was, they'd have to wait it out. In the meantime, they were hoping to get a hit on the car Yousefi was driving so they could at least keep an eye on him until the meet, as well, but he could've already ditched the car. There was simply no way to know at the moment.

Sebastian turned as I walked out of the bathroom. "I'll call you back," he said, hanging up before the other person had a chance to respond. "It's a little big." He pointed to his T-shirt, the one with the Harley Davidson logo on it.

"It'll do." Suddenly self-conscious, I walked to the bed, climbed in, and pulled the covers up to my ears.

My braid hung wet down my back, making me cold even in the well-heated cabin. Sebastian had started a fire to dry out his duster and the scent of burning pine permeated the air around me. It smelled heavenly.

"I guess I'm next." He grabbed some clothes out of a satchel and a towel off a hook by the fire. "Did you leave any hot water?"

"No," I teased. "But if you hadn't kept barging in, it wouldn't have taken me so long to finish up. Good thing the shower curtain is opaque."

He allowed the barest hint of a rather sad smile to cross his features. "I just want you to know, I'm truly grateful for all your help."

"Thank you," I said, surprised.

He nodded and started for the bathroom again. Just before he closed the door behind him, he said, "And, just for the record, it's not completely opaque." He closed the door against the sound of my gasp.

I couldn't decide if I should be flattered or appalled. In his defense, I stared at him for a solid ten minutes while I'd paused time not one hour ago. Was this any different?

Yes!

Yes, it was. At least he wasn't naked.

Suddenly, I had nothing to do. I wanted to read but had no book. No magazine. Not even a cereal box. And since Chicago PD had never given me back my phone, an oversight that would be addressed very soon, I couldn't even check my email.

Then again, who was I kidding? The only person who emailed me was my neighbor Mindy, and that was only to tell me about the latest UFO sightings around the globe. That crap was like crack to her, mostly because, according to her, she'd been abducted when she was a child. She told me once her abduction had given her powers of observation and that was how she knew I was *special.* She added air quotes for effect.

But as much of an annoyance as she was, I missed her. Mindy would be worried, too. She kept telling me the government would come for me. They'd want to open me up and dissect me. A morbid thought. I'd never told her what I could do, but she still knew I could manipulate time. She said it was in my eyes. I had the eyes of an old traveler who could never rest in one place for very long.

She was stark-raving nuts, but I liked her, and I missed not knowing the latest on UFO sightings. I'd be so behind when I got back.

Since I had absolutely nothing else to do, and the thought of Sebastian all naked only a few feet away from me was making me lightheaded, I decided to drop, if for no other reason than to see what a special agent does while undercover.

I bent my head and jumped into the warm water of time as it reversed around me. After reaching the limit I stopped, and it didn't take long for something very interesting to happen.

Sebastian was shirtless, for one thing, standing at the door, the lean muscle of his back flexing with every move. He wore leather chaps over his jeans and leather armbands around his wrists. That took me a moment to get over. The next thing was the fact that a rather trashy-looking brunette was standing on the other side of the threshold, trying to talk her way into Sebastian's room.

"What are you doing here, Jenny?" he asked her.

"I saw you at the clubhouse," she said with a pretty shrug. "Can you believe we both ended up in the same place after all these years? Thought I'd say hello for old times' sake. See if you wanted to catch up."

"Aren't you exclusively Corte's?"

Corte, the club member that Vince, along with Sebastian, didn't trust.

"Please," she said. "That pig passed out hours ago. This is between you—" She ran her index finger in a circle on his chest, just in case her intentions weren't quite clear enough. "—and me."

"Corte's a friend."

"Corte's an ass."

He took a swig from the beer he was holding, and I realized there were several bottles on the ground around the trashcan, as though he missed but didn't care enough to rectify the situation.

"So, what happened to you?" she purred as she let her fingers walk up his chest playfully. "You had so much promise in high school. Quarterback. Captain of the football team. Everyone thought you'd go pro after Notre Dame."

"I blew out my knee senior year."

"Oh, right," she said, nodding in remembrance. "Too bad. You had a killer handoff. Wait." She stopped her flirtations and straightened. "Didn't you go to Langley or something?"

Sebastian took the last swig of the beer he was holding, tossed it in—or very near—the trashcan, then crossed his arms over his chest to lean against the doorframe.

"Yeah. Yeah, you did. I remember your mom bragging about it to my grandma, like you were going to be somebody and the rest of us were dog excrement."

"Langley didn't really work out, either."

"You're just full of great intentions, aren't you, love? Either way, Vince won't look kindly upon your chosen profession, dropout or not. I could tell him everything I know about you. Might even score Corte some brownie points with the boss."

"What do you want?"

"What I've always wanted." She closed the distance between them. "You."

Sadly, I was right there with her.

"You're drunk, Jenny. Go home."

She threw her arms around his neck. "I just want you once, Sebastian. Or is it Sam?"

Sam must've been Sebastian's undercover name. While I could understand her desire, no meant no. And she was threatening a very good friend of mine, no matter that I'd only known him a little over 17 hours. And we got off to a rocky start.

"I've wanted you since I was in the second grade."

A tad longer than I'd wanted him, but still.

He disentangled her limbs, even her lower ones, but she fought him. She pulled his hair then slapped him with a powerful force, the sound echoing against the quiet backdrop of night.

"Fine," she said, her feelings hurt. "I just hope Vince doesn't mind that you were going to be a fed." She glared up at him, spitting out every word. "Hell, who knows? Maybe you still are."

He grabbed her from behind when she started to walk away, dragged her into his room, and shoved her against the wall. The Cheshire smile she wore confirmed Sebastian's actions were exactly what she wanted from him.

He crushed her with his body, his rough kisses making her moan and grind against him. He pushed open the leather vest she wore and her bare breasts bounced out to meet his palms. He cupped one with one hand while pushing her jeans down with the other.

There was something primal about his movements. Something raw. I looked away and realized his phone was still backlit. He hadn't relocked it. Dangerous considering who was at the door. I walked over and read the message still displayed on the screen.

Yes, it has been confirmed. Cham died this afternoon. Investigation underway. Will be in touch. TG

Had he just found out about his partner? My hands flew to my mouth as I watched him. That would explain his harsh treatment of Jenny, not that she didn't give as good as she got. For every punishment he doled out, she retaliated with a sharp scratch of her nails or a stinging nip with her teeth.

I glanced down. I shouldn't be watching something so

private. Something so personal for Sebastian. He was clearly in pain. Maybe a tryst with Jenny was exactly what he needed. And yet, I couldn't leave. Knowing he was suffering, he was hurting and in turn trying to hurt Jenny, I just couldn't leave him.

He finally got her jeans off and pushed his own pants, along with the chaps, halfway to his knees. Then he tore open a condom wrapper he'd dug out of his pocket and rolled it onto his hard cock. It was the sexiest thing I'd ever seen.

I turned my back to them, but I could still see everything reflecting in the window. I watched as he drove into her, as her head flew back, as she moaned in ecstasy, begging him to go harder. He obeyed. He grabbed hold of a window frame beside him for leverage with one hand and her hair with the other and thrust into her with all the pain and anger he had.

I dipped my head and closed my eyes, realizing I should not be there on a thousand levels, but I wanted to make sure Jenny had been appeased. I wanted to make sure she wouldn't tell her boyfriend or her boyfriend's boss about Sebastian. I wanted to make sure he was safe.

The groan coming from Sebastian when he came rushed over me like wildfire. It weakened my knees and if I had really been in the room, I would've needed to sit down before I collapsed. Jenny's scream didn't take away from the deep, guttural growl coming from her conquest.

Heavy panting filled the room a moment later, and I heard the springs give on the bed.

"Now, *that's* what I'm talking about," Jenny said.

I barely turned to see Sebastian fasten his pants in my periphery.

"Don't put that bad boy away just yet," she said, grabbing his wrist and pulling him toward her. "I'd bet my last dollar he has a couple more of those in him before the night is through."

He didn't lie down as she'd wanted. Instead, he hiked a knee on the bed beside her, took a T-shirt, and began tearing it into strips.

"I like where this is headed," she purred, crossing her wrists above her head.

He straddled her, pulling her wrists toward him to tie them together. She was naked except for the vest that lay open, and she was absolutely lovely. No wonder she scored an exclusive in a motorcycle club. Most women were fair game for one and all. I couldn't blame Sebastian for taking advantage of the situation, especially in his condition.

He lifted her onto her feet and turned her to face the wall. Her hands still above her head, he kneeled and tied her ankles together as well.

"Okay," she said, completely clueless, because this could only end one way. I saw that now. "I don't normally allow that route, but if it's the back door you want, then the back door you'll get. You have to promise to fight for me, though. Corte won't take this lying down."

He finished tying the knot, then stood behind her, pressing his body into hers.

"Promise?" she asked again, waiting for a commitment out of him.

Instead of promising her the moon, he wrapped a hand around her waist and lifted her into his arms.

At first, she was very into it. She squirmed with delight until he carried her to the large window that looked out into the forest. The large window that was now open.

"What are you doing?" she asked when he lifted her toward the opening.

"Keep her detained until all this is over."

A man was there dressed entirely in black. "Yes, sir. Does she maybe have clothes?"

"I'll get them. Hold on."

"What the hell?" she screamed. The man who took her slammed a hand over her mouth, but she continued to yell past his gloved fingers.

"You rat bastard. You didn't have to fuck me. You could have taken me away at any time, if that was your plan."

"Not at all," Sebastian said, tossing her belongings to another man who emerged from the shadows. "I had to keep you entertained until the guy Vince set to watch me fell asleep. The fuck was completely necessary." He pointed to the front window as though he could see his guard past the darkness.

She kicked furiously, and I couldn't help but admire her spunk. In truth, I felt she gave him little choice.

The guy who caught the clothes hurried up to grab the woman's legs. He paused and offered Sebastian his sympathies. "I'm so sorry about your partner, sir."

"Thanks, Danvers. Watch her left hook."

The men chuckled and absconded with her into the night. I wondered how much they saw of the tryst beforehand. Sebastian certainly didn't seem worried.

His phone rang as he started unfastening his pants again. He answered it with a simple, "Yes."

I eased close to hear the call.

"We got her," a male on the other end said. "The girl sending the notes. She's being held in Chicago, and they've had her for almost three days. You should get over here, if you can."

"I'm in the middle of something," he said, his face lined with exhaustion. I could feel the weight of his anger, of the sorrow he felt with his partner's passing.

"I think you were right about her, Strand. She's different."

I recognized the man's voice. It was the deputy secretary.

"I'll be on the next flight."

"Forget that. I'm sending a chopper. Can you get away?"

"Yeah. Everyone's asleep. I'll take the truck to the rendezvous. No one will notice."

"I'll have it there in thirty."

CHAPTER 7

Sebastian hung up and showered quickly. I didn't look in on him. Not that first time, anyway. I fast-forwarded until I was almost at the present. Sebastian was in the shower again. This time I risked a quick peek. He was right. The curtain wasn't opaque, but nothing was opaque in this realm. I watched as water sheeted over his wide shoulders, down his back and over his delicious ass.

He turned off the shower and pulled back the curtain to reach for his towel. I watched unabashedly as he wiped steam off the mirror with the towel, standing gloriously naked. I was abusing my power on so many levels, but I just had to try one last thing. I walked forward and ran my hand down his back. I could almost feel him. The smoothness of his skin. The bunching of his muscles. When my hand met a steely buttock, it kept going, caressing the curve, marveling at the dip that lined his hips, the divot in his shapely buttocks.

I would probably never see him again after tonight, but I most definitely would never forget him. I was even considering a career in law enforcement. Perhaps I'd go to Langley. Nah. The CIA gave a psych eval before they hired. I'd never pass. I might make a good cop though. I'd never considered it before now.

I felt the pull of the present. I must've been close. With one last look, I released time the second I noticed Sebastian had stopped what he was doing. He'd turned as though looking for something. As though looking for someone.

My eyes flew open as Sebastian bolted through the door. He paused, scanned the area with a wary expression, then planted his cerulean gaze on me. His hair hung in thick, wet clumps around his face. He raked a hand through it, slicking it back but only for a moment before it fell forward again.

I raised my brows in utter innocence. While he held the towel in front of the most pertinent parts of himself, the dips in the hips were still clearly evident. As were his killer abs.

"Did you feel something?" he asked me.

"No." Gawd I was such a good liar.

He furrowed his brows then nodded, not quite convinced as he closed the door behind him again.

The close call had my heart racing, but had he felt me? There was simply no way. The very idea was impossible. When I dropped, I wasn't really there. I wasn't really corporeal. How—?

The door opened again. This time he wore the towel around his waist, the image just as jaw-droppingly sexy as before. He'd slicked back his hair and I got to see more of the angles and lines of his handsome face. His masculinity would never be in question.

He narrowed his lashes at me in suspicion. "Are you sure you didn't feel anything?"

"Yep," I said, barely able to rip my gaze off the towel. It could drop at any moment. I didn't want to miss the show.

He stepped around the bed and sat on the edge of it. The freshly showered scent of him filled the room and made me heady. His arms, so beautifully woven, rested on his knees and he gazed at me from underneath wet lashes spiked with water from the shower.

"Are you okay?" he asked.

"Absolutely," I said a little too enthusiastically.

Understanding flooded his expression. "You dropped, didn't you?"

"What?" I asked, appalled. "I beg your pardon."

He stood and turned his back to me. "How much did you see?"

I bit my lower lip until I tasted a drop of blood. "Not much. Really. There wasn't anything to see."

After a quick scoff, he lowered his head. "This is what I do, Andrea. I detect lies, and I'm the best, I promise you. It's how I've gotten so far so fast."

His admission had me wondering if he didn't have a touch of something supernatural himself.

He pressed his mouth together as though in regret. "She's okay. She's being detained at a local facility until all this is over. That's all."

I nodded. "I shouldn't have invaded your privacy so blatantly. I…I didn't watch."

He laid a humorless grin on me. "I detect lies."

"I didn't watch everything." Humiliation surged through me, heating my face until I was sure it shone scarlet. "I'm sorry."

He was angry, and I'd just lost what little trust I'd gained from him with that one, stupid drop. But it didn't stop him from being curious.

"How do you do it?" he asked as he sat down beside me again. "How on earth can you see things that have already happened?"

With a one-shouldered shrug, I said, "I have no idea. We can just do it."

"We?"

His nearness was warming me even further. I wanted to scoot away from him, but only because his proximity made me ache to reach out and touch him. I wanted to lace my fingers into this. I wanted to run the back of my hand down his arm. I wanted to trace the hills and valleys of his biceps with my fingertips. Or my tongue. Either way. It made me a little pathetic to want him so badly, and I grew more embarrassed with the thought.

"The women in my family. We've been dropping since before my great-great-grandmother. She was in the circus. Her boss used her to get information about people so he could extort money from them. My great-grandmother was killed by a man who thought she was possessed. My grandmother and her twin sister were practically hermits. No one really knows what happened to them, what made them so afraid of the world. They were quite popular when they were young, but as they got older, they became a little touched."

"Touched?" he asked.

"Insane."

He shifted even closer and my desire to touch him grew exponentially. I crossed my arms over my chest to keep from acting on said desire.

"And your mother?"

I glanced away, embarrassed. "She got mixed up with organized crime somehow. She showed her gift to the wrong person, trusted the wrong man, and ended up doing unspeakable things."

"Like what?" he asked, his voice still a touch harsh.

He would probably never trust me again, and the thought broke my heart.

"I have no idea. She never told me. All I remember is growing up with an alcoholic, emotionally absent mother. But she left me a house," I said, ending the tragic story on a happy note.

"How long have you been able to do it? To drop?"

"Since I was little. My mother taught me."

He sat back in contemplation. "What was it like growing up with this?"

"It's the wrong kind of power for a kid."

He lifted my chin so I had to look at him. "I'm sorry, Andi."

I sucked in a soft breath. He called me Andi. Mindy, my crazy friend who'd been abducted by aliens as a child, said that the man I would fall in love with would call me Andi. Damn, did she ever nail that one. Too bad I'd probably never see him again after this case was solved.

His gaze dropped to my mouth and my whole body vibrated with want. I'd never felt anything like it. He ran his thumb over my bottom lip and time stood still. Metaphorically.

The alarming sound of his phone chirping startled me out of my euphoric state. As though he regretted doing so, he dropped his hand and stood to get the phone, swiping it off the table impatiently.

"Yes," he said, his voice suddenly brusque. After a moment, he walked back into the bathroom for some privacy. Did he learn nothing? I could totally drop and listen to the entire conversation at will. But I refrained. Best to get rid of such bad habits before they spiraled out of control. Nip them in the bud, as Mindy would say.

After a few moments, Sebastian came back out. This time he was wearing a fresh pair of loose jeans. But nothing else. No socks. No shirt. Holy mother of—

"They found it," he said, sitting beside me again. The bed dipped with his weight. It seemed even gravity wanted me closer to him.

I drew my knees to my chest. It was a defensive maneuver. I was defending him against me. "That's great."

He chuckled softly. "Do you know what I'm talking about?"

"Not so much, but it sounds like good news."

"It is. Very. And it's all thanks to you."

"That's a plus. I'm not usually on the ingratiating side of the table."

"They found the chemical bomb."

I bolted upright. "They found it? How?"

"Based on the description you gave, they realized the drop was actually going to be tomorrow. Midday Eucharist at that church is on Thursdays. That didn't give them much time, so they went in to install surveillance cameras tonight and found the device by accident. Vince had already stashed it there so no one would find him with it."

"And they're sure it's the only one?"

"We know the Disciples were only bringing one into the country. But we should know more soon. They have Vince in custody and, thanks again to your description of the vehicle, Yousefi as well. He was pulled over in Albany for a missing taillight and brought in for driving a stolen car."

"No way." I couldn't believe it, how easily it all came together. "This…this is—" I had no words, but for the first time since I'd met him, Sebastian flashed a huge, bright smile at me.

"Amazing," he offered.

I flew forward and wrapped my arms around him. Relief that he would be okay washed over me. He encircled me in his arms, his hold solid, his embrace warm.

"We're not really sure what to do with you," he said into my hair.

I leaned back. "What do you mean?"

A playful grin tugged at the corner of his mouth. Gawd I loved that tug.

"On one hand," he said, "you're a threat to national security."

My jaw dropped. "How am I a threat to national security?"

"You could stand outside the White House and listen in to everything that happens there. Do you know what you could do with that information?"

"Not especially."

"Good," he said, a sexy smile in his voice. "On the other," he continued, "you could be an incredible asset."

"I charge by the hour," I teased. "And I demand benefits." No matter that the benefit I most desired was him. In the back of my mind, I realized I could be locked up tomorrow. Once they considered all of the implications of my ability, I truly would be a threat to national security. I'd never thought of it that way, but he was right. Wonderful. I really could be sent for an extended stay at Gitmo.

After a long moment, he grinned. "I have a feeling you could demand anything your heart desires."

Those were so the wrong words.

"My boss is quite taken with you."

"Good to know. I've had my eye on a jet for a while."

"They're coming for you, now."

I scooted back away from him. "Now? But I thought—"

"Yeah, well, since this is over, they see no reason for you to be stuck here with me."

He stood and started to grab my things. "I'm being shipped to headquarters for debriefing and my new assignment."

"Oh," I said, my heart shattering. I was honestly the most pathetic being on the planet. I stood and helped him, not that I had much. Or, well, anything but a couple articles of clothing. "Are they going to bring my clothes back?"

"They didn't say. Frankly, I like the look."

I snatched the blouse I'd worn for three days out of his hands and glanced around the room. "Why did they take my pants and not my blouse? And where's my jacket?"

"Being cleaned. It was covered in mud as well."

I was trying to stay busy, but I had nothing to do. I had to leave. I was going away and would probably never see him again and it broke my heart. How could I have gotten so attached to someone in so short a time?

My chest constricted painfully as I studied my blouse. Sebastian walked up behind me, close behind me, until his body was pressed into mine. "I would like to see you again," he said, his voice husky.

Holy mother of Hades. I didn't dare move. He'd placed his hands on my hips and buried his face in my hair. How could he even like me? How could he want to be so near me? Men didn't like me. The last thing they wanted was to be near me. I had orange hair and dark freckles and a strange personality.

While a part of me wanted to analyze the situation like I always did, another part wanted to pull him closer. That part won out. I reached back, grabbed hold of his jeans, and pulled until his crotch was at my back and there was no longer any doubt how he felt about me. He molded himself to my backside, his erection filling the small of my back.

He wrapped a hand around my throat and guided my face up to his where he kissed me. There was no hesitation in the act. His kiss was deep and dark and desperate, not at all like he kissed Jenny, and his taste was alluring and primal.

He deepened the kiss, driving harder into my mouth as his free hand pulled the borrowed T-shirt up to the top of the boxers. Without breaking the kiss, he slid his hand inside.

My stomach lurched with anticipation. Pleasure pooled in my abdomen, hot and pulsating as his fingers slid so close, so very close. Then he cursed into my mouth and pulled away.

I wanted to scream. I turned to him, ready to plead with him to continue, but he put several feet between us, running his fingers through his hair.

"I'm sorry," he said, his voice raw with desire. "You're an asset. I'm breaking all kinds of ethics, not to mention a few laws."

I stood panting, clutching the boxers to my abdomen, afraid they would fall if I didn't.

"I should not have done that, and I apologize."

"It's okay," I said, wondering if he'd simply changed his mind and was using ethics and laws as an excuse. I searched for my blouse again. "It's okay. I understand."

"No, you don't." He walked back and placed his hands on my shoulders. "You have no…no idea."

He gasped and it took me a moment to realize he was struggling to breathe. I was so wrapped up in what he was going to say, I only noticed the crimson pouring down his chest after he grabbed it. Then the sound I'd heard in the back of my mind registered. A ping, like something hitting glass. Shattering it.

He'd been shot. A scream that started in the deepest part of my being wrenched free and echoed in the room as another shot sent Sebastian to his knees. I collapsed onto him, covering his body as best I could, screaming as loud as I could for help.

While the man who walked up to the large plate glass window that faced the woods was the geek, Yousefi's tech guy, all I saw was Travis, the kid who'd shot the Padgetts 24 hours earlier. He held a sniper rifle in one hand and drew a pistol with the other. Just like Travis, this guy showed no emotion whatsoever. He aimed the pistol at my head and pulled the trigger.

CHAPTER 8

In that instant, a moment of utter clarity took hold. I'd dropped, and it took me a few seconds to realize that the instant I reentered my body, I would die.

I would die.

I rewound time a few, precious minutes. I watched as Sebastian led my mouth to his. As he plunged his tongue inside me. As he caressed my neck and chin to hold me to him.

The beauty of his face stunned me. He was so sensual. So alluring. So desperate. It hurt to watch. To know what was about to happen. There had to be a way to save him.

I looked past the two of us and out the window of the cabin. A glint of moonlight caught my eye. I squinted and saw the tech guy pulling the butt of a rifle into his shoulder. He leaned over the barrel, lining Sebastian up in his crosshairs.

I had to stop it. There had to be a way.

I looked back at the two of us as Sebastian tore himself away from me. I could get to him. There was still time. Maybe I could warn him somehow. He'd felt me before. I knew it. But nothing I could do would warn him of what awaited him.

I turned back to myself. I was there. Right there. I'd entered my body at a different time once and only once before. When I'd gotten lost for what seemed like years, I'd found myself in a coma and was able to reenter. But that had been in the future and the weeks, possibly years, I spent in the oblivion of time changed me. I wasn't the same person when I came out as when I'd gone in.

But I had to try. If I caused a rift in the universe, so be it. Sebastian Strand was definitely worth the risk. I rewound time to the second Sebastian broke off the kiss, then I stepped into myself, into my body. Could I reenter in the past?

I glanced at Sebastian, at the pain and regret in his handsome face, and I released time, but I controlled it. Shaped it. Bent it to my will. I forced it back to where I stood.

The warm water evaporated as I compelled each and every molecule in my body to remain in that moment. It was like fighting gravity itself, and gravity was a WWE wrestler while I'd merely dabbled in shadowboxing. It was winning. I felt myself being snapped back to when I'd dropped and panic shot through me.

I wouldn't get a second chance. That bullet would tear through my brain and it would be over in an instant. I gritted my teeth and fought harder against the tide. And then, as though everything clicked into place, it folded. Time came to me instead of me going to it.

Realizing I was in a different place than when I started the drop, I opened my eyes just as I turned to look at him. Stunned I'd done it. Stunned it'd worked. Stunned I didn't have a bullet ripping through my brain at that moment.

I snapped to attention, sprinted forward and, catching him unaware, tackled him to the ground. He stared at me as though I'd lost my mind. I got that a lot. But I pointed toward the window and whispered one word.

"Sniper!"

Without a hint of hesitation, he dragged me across the floor, using the bed as cover, and dug his pistol out of a duffle bag. Then he flattened against the carpet and slid under the bed, pulling me with him. I'd grabbed his phone. He took it, unlocked it with his thumbprint, and handed it back to me, all without taking his eyes off the window.

I started scrolling through his contacts before realizing I had no idea who to call.

"Danvers," he said without looking back at me. "Call Danvers." He kept his gaze locked, waiting for the sniper to show himself.

I found Danvers in his contacts and dialed the number. "Yes," he said, exactly like Sebastian did when he answered the phone. I guess they could never be sure who was on the other end.

"We have a sniper," I whispered into the phone. Not sure why. "Behind Agent Strand's room in the woods."

"Understood."

The call ended before I could say anything else, but it didn't take the sniper long to figure out we were on to him. I dropped and watched him circle the cabin to the front.

"He went around," I said the second I released time, and Sebastian immediately pulled me farther under the bed, rolling onto his knees on the other side and using the bed as cover.

I dropped again. "He'll be at that window in two seconds."

Then I heard a shot. And another. Three more split the air until my ears were ringing and, unable to wait another second, I scrambled out from under the bed to examine my protector. No holes.

Danvers crashed into the room with gun drawn, but Sebastian gave him the all-clear signal.

"You sure there's only the one?" he asked, and Sebastian gazed at me in question.

I dropped again and searched the entire area before popping back into the present. "That's all I can see."

"We need to get you to safety regardless, sir, while I call this in."

Sebastian didn't hear him. Or he didn't listen. He was too busy studying me. "Andi, how did you know?"

The reality of the situation hit me so hard, I struggled to breathe under the weight of it. "He shot you," I said, almost passing out with the thought. "He shot you. Twice. I tried to protect you, but he was going to shoot me in the head. And... and you were already gone." My hands flew to my mouth in anguish as a sob ripped through my chest.

Sebastian pulled me to him roughly. And he believed me. He never doubted anything I said. Who does that?

An hour later, we were surrounded by the flashing lights of a dozen cop cars when Deputy Secretary Gill pulled up in a black SUV. He stepped out, adjusted his jacket, then walked up to us as we sat on the porch sharing a blanket.

"I take it you're okay?" he asked Sebastian.

"Thanks to Andrea."

He sat down beside me, his face grave. "I've thought long and hard about your situation, Ms. Grace."

"Just Andrea, please."

"Andrea. If people find out about you, even people in my own department, you'll be in danger. Some will see you as a risk to national security. Some will try to exploit your gift for their own gain. And some will try to have you locked away for the rest of your life."

I nodded, understanding all too well.

"That's why I'd like to invite you to be a part of a special investigations team headed by the new director, Special Agent Sebastian Strand."

I glanced at Sebastian, who was just as surprised as I was. "Sir, I don't think—"

"Strand, you are every bit ready."

Sebastian thought about the impromptu offer, then looked down at me. "I hear your new boss is a bit of an ass."

"Now, now," Gill said. "I only called you that one time, and you deserved it."

"I did," Sebastian told me. "He's right."

The older man knelt in front of us. "We'd love to have you on our side, Andrea."

"I need to learn a lot more if I'm going to do this."

"I'm sure Agent Strand can help with that. Yours is a very special talent. I have a feeling you'll be teaching us a few things."

"I'd love to," I said, feeling for the first time like my life had purpose.

"Wonderful. We'll get on this immediately." He stood and started to walk away when he turned back to us. "And I'd like to remind you about our strict non-fraternization policy."

My eyes rounded, and Gill chuckled as he walked back to his waiting ride.

"For real?" I asked Sebastian.

"Hey, he did just appoint me the head of the unit. I bet we can bend the rules a little."

I placed a serious gaze on him, because it was time to get serious, in my humble, inexperienced opinion. "I've only had sex one time in my whole life."

He blinked in surprise. "And how'd that work out for you?"

"It was awful. I want good sex."

Fighting a grin, he said, "We'll put that in your contract under benefits."

"Works for me," I said as we watched the horizon turn pink with the promise of dawn. "And I want my watch back. And my phone. And I need to know that my panties are okay." I loved those panties.

"Just hold on, now. Let's not get carried away. The department cannot be held responsible for the state of your undergarments." His gaze grew serious and something deep inside me stirred when he added, "But we do have a dress code. I'll need to perform regular checks."

I gasped as he wrapped the blanket around us tighter, but not because of the cold. He apparently decided to check the state of my undergarments right then and there. I fought to stay still as a blistering heat flooded my nether regions.

When he leaned down and whispered into my ear, "Spread your legs, Agent Grace," my world turned upside down and inside out and I knew I had finally found a place in the world. Right beside Director Sebastian Strand.

Please enjoy this sneak peek from A Bad Day for Sunshine, the first in the Sunshine Vicram Series!

A

BAD DAY

FOR

SUNSHINE

CHAPTER 1

Welcome to Del Sol,
A town full of sunshine,
fresh air, and friendly faces.
(Barring three or four old grouches.)

Sunshine Vicram pushed down the dread and sticky knot of angst in her chest and wondered, yet again, if she were ready to be sheriff of a town even the locals called the Psych Ward. Del Sol, New Mexico. The town she grew up in. The town she'd abandoned. The town that held more secrets than a politician's wife.

Was she having second thoughts? Now? After all the hubbub and hoopla of winning an election she hadn't even entered?

Hell yes, she was.

But after her night of debauchery—a.k.a. her last hurrah before the town became her responsibility—she thought she'd conquered her fears. Eviscerated them. Beaten and buried them in the dirt of the Sangre de Cristo Mountains.

Either Jose Cuervo had lied to her last night and given her a false sense of security, or her morning cup of joe was affecting her more than she thought possible.

She eyed the cup suspiciously and took another sip before looking out the kitchen window toward the trees in the distance. The snow had stopped last night, but it had restarted with the first rays of dawn. Snow storms weren't uncommon in New Mexico, especially in the more mountainous regions, but Sun had been hoping for, well, sun her first day on the job. Still, snow or no snow, nothing could stop the brilliance that awaited her along the horizon.

Thick clouds soaked up the vibrant colors of daybreak and splashed them across the heavens like a manic artist who'd scored a new bottle of Adderall. Orange Crush and cotton candy collided and dovetailed, making the sky look like a watercolor that had been left out in the rain. The vibrant hues reflected off the fat flakes drifting down and powdering the landscape.

Sun was home. After almost fifteen years, she was home.

But for how long?

No. That wasn't the right question. Somewhere between her karaoke rendition of "Who Let the Dogs Out?"—which bordered on genius—and her fifth shot of tequila, she and Jose had figured that out the night before as well.

This was the opportunity she'd been both anticipating and dreading. Since she had a job handed to her on a silver platter, she would stay until she found the man who'd abducted her when she was seventeen. She would stay until he was prosecuted to the fullest extent of the law. She would stay until she could shed light on the darkest event of her life, and then she would put the town in her rearview for good.

The right question was not how long she would stay but

how long it would take her to bring her worst nightmare—literally—to justice.

She tucked a strand of blond hair behind her ear and appraised the *guesthouse* her parents had built, studying it for the umpteenth time that morning. The Tuscan two-bedroom felt bigger than it was thanks to the vaulted ceilings and large windows.

All things considered, it wasn't bad. Not bad at all. It was shiny and new and warm. And the fact that it sat on her parents' property, barely fifty feet from their back door, was surprisingly reassuring.

She'd worked some long hours as a detective. Surely, as a sheriff, that wouldn't change. It may even get worse. It would be good to know that Auri, the effervescent fruit of her loins, would be safe.

The kid felt as much at home in the small tourist town as Sun did, having spent every summer in Del Sol with her grandparents since she was two. The fact that she'd twirled through the apartment when they first saw it like a drunken ballerina? Also a strong indicator she would be okay.

Auri loved it, just like Cyrus and Elaine Freyr knew she would. Sun's parents were nothing if not determined.

And that brought her back to the malfeasance at hand. They were living in an apartment her parents had built. An apartment her parents had built specifically for Sun and Auri despite their insistence it was *simply a guesthouse.* They didn't have guests. At least, not guests that stayed overnight. The apartment was just one more clue they'd been planning this ambush for a very long time.

They'd wanted her back in Del Sol. Sun had known that since the day she'd left with baby in hand and resentment in heart. Not toward her parents. What happened had not been their fault. The resentment that had been eating away at her for years stemmed from a tiff with life in general. Sometimes the hand you're dealt sucks.

But if she were honest with herself—and she liked to think she was—the agonizing torment of unrequited love may have played a teensy-tiny part.

So, she ran, much like an addled schoolgirl, though she didn't go far. Also, much like an addled schoolgirl.

She'd originally fled to Albuquerque, only an hour and a half from Del Sol. But she'd moved to Santa Fe a few years ago, first as an officer, then as a detective for SFPD. She'd only been thirty minutes from her parents, and she'd hoped the proximity would make her abandonment of all things Del Sol easier on them.

It hadn't. And now Sun would pay the price for their audacity, their desperate attempt to pull her back into the fold. As would Auri. The fact that they didn't take Auri's future into consideration when coming up with their scheme irked. Just enough to cause tiny bouts of hyperventilation every time Sun thought about it.

Auri's voice drifted toward her, lyrical and airy like the bubbles in champagne. "It looks good on you."

Sun turned. Her daughter, short and yet somehow taller than she had a right to be at fourteen, stood in the doorway to her room, tucking a T-shirt into a pair of jeans and gesturing to Sun's uniform.

Instead of acknowledging the compliment, Sun took a moment to admire the girl who'd stolen her heart about three seconds after she was born. Which happened to be about two seconds before Sun had declared the newborn the most beautiful thing this world had ever seen.

Then again, Sunshine had just given birth to a six-pound velociraptor. Her judgment could've been skewed.

Though not likely. The girl had inherited the ability to stop a train in its tracks by the time she was two. Her looks were unusual enough to be considered surreal. Sadly, she owed none of her features to Sunshine. Or her grandparents, for that matter.

Auri's hair hung in thick, coppery waves down her back. Sunshine's hair hung in a tangled mess of blond with mousy brown undertones when it wasn't French braided, as it was now.

Auri's hazel eyes glistened like a penny, a freshly minted one around the depths of her pupils and an aged one that had green patina around the edges. Sun's were a murky cobalt blue, much like her grandmother's collection of vintage Milk of Magnesia bottles.

Auri's skin had been infused with the natural glow of someone who spent a lot of time outdoors. Sunshine was about as tan as notebook paper.

The girl seemed to have inherited everything from her father. A fact that chafed.

"Mom," Auri said, pursing her pouty lips, "you're doing it again."

Sun snapped out of her musings and gave her daughter a sheepish grin from behind the cup. "Sorry."

She dropped her gaze to the spiffy new uniform she'd donned that morning. As the newest sheriff of Del Sol County, Sun got to choose the colors she and her deputies would wear. For both their tactical and dress uniforms, she chose black. Sharp. Mysterious. Slightly menacing.

And because she wanted to look her best first day on the job, she'd opted for the Class A. Her dress uniform. She ran her fingertips over the badge pinned above the front pocket of her button-down. Inspected the embroidered sheriff's patch on her shoulder. Marveled at how slimming black trousers really were.

"I do look rather badass, don't I?"

Auri adjusted the waist of her jeans and offered a patient smile. "All that matters is that *you* think you look badass."

"Yeah, well, it's still crazy. And if I'm not mistaken, illegal on several levels." How her parents got her elected as sheriff when she'd had no idea she was even running was only one of many mysteries the peculiar town of Del Sol had to offer. "Your grandparents are definitely going to prison for this. And so am I, most likely, so enjoy my badassery while it lasts."

"Mom!" Auri threw her hands over her ears. "I can't hear that."

"Badassery?" she asked, confused. "You've heard so much worse. Remember when that guy pulled out in front of me on Cerrillos? Heavy flow day." She pointed to herself. "Not to be messed with."

"Grandma and Grandpa won't go to prison. They're too old."

Unfortunately, they were not too old. Not by a long shot. "Election tampering is a serious offense."

"They didn't tamper. They just, you know, wriggled."

Sun's expression flatlined. "I'll be sure to tell the judge that. Hopefully before I'm sentenced."

Auri had been about to grab her sweater when she threw her hands over her ears again. "Mom!" she said, her chastising glare the stuff of legend. The stuff that could melt the faces off a death squad at fifty yards. Because there were so many of those nowadays. "You can't go to prison, either. You'll never survive. They'll smell cop all over you and force you to be Big Betty's bitch before they shank you in the showers."

She'd put a lot of thought into this.

Sun set down the cup, walked to her daughter, and placed her hands on the teen's shoulders, her expression set to one of sympathy and understanding. "You need to hear this, hon.

You're going to have to fend for yourself soon. Just remember, you gave at the office, never wear a thong on a first date, and when in doubt, throw it out."

Auri paused before asking, "What does that even mean?"

"I don't know. It's just always worked for me." She walked back to her coffee, took a sip, grimaced, and stuck the cup into the microwave.

"Grandma and Grandpa can't go to jail."

Sun turned back to her fiery offspring and crossed her arms over her chest, refusing to acknowledge the apprehension gnawing at her gut. "It would serve them right."

"No, Mom," she said as she pulled a sweater over her head. "It wouldn't."

Sun dropped her gaze. "Well, then, it would serve me right, I suppose." The microwave beeped. She took out her cup and blew softly, having left it in long enough to scald several layers off her tongue, as usual. "But first I have to check out my new office."

While she'd been sworn in and taken office on January 1, she had yet to step foot inside the station that would be her home away from home until the next election in four years. Barring coerced resignation.

She and Auri had taken an extra week to get moved in after the holidays. To prepare for their new lives. To gird their loins, so to speak.

"I need to decorate it," she continued, losing herself in thought. "You know, make the new digs my own. Do you think I should put up my Hello Kitty clock? Would it send the wrong message?"

"Yes. Well?" Auri stood up straight to give her mother an unimpeded view. She wore a rust-colored sweater, stretchy denim jeans, and a pair of brown boots that buckled up the sides. The colors looked stunning against her coppery hair and sun-kissed skin.

She did a 360 so Sun could get a better look.

Sun lowered her cup. "You look amazing."

Auri gave a half-hearted grin, walked to her, and took the coffee out of her mother's hands. That kid drank more coffee than she did. Warning her it would stunt her growth had done nothing to assuage the girl's enthusiasm over the years. Sun was so proud.

"Are you nervous?" she asked.

Auri lifted a shoulder and downed half the cup before answering, "No. I don't know. Maybe."

"You are definitely my daughter. Indecisiveness runs in the family."

"It's weird, though. Real clothes."

Auri had been in private school her entire life. She'd loved the academy in Santa Fe, but she'd been excited about the move regardless. At least, she had up until a few days ago. Sun had sensed a change. A withdrawal. Auri swore it was all in her mother's overprotective gray matter, but Sun knew her daughter too well to dismiss her misgivings.

She'd sensed that same kind of withdrawal when Auri was seven, but she'd ignored her maternal instincts. That decision almost cost Auri her life. She would not make that mistake again.

"You know, you can still go back to the academy. It's only—"

"Thirty minutes away. I know." Auri handed back the cup and grabbed her coat, and Sun couldn't help but notice a hint of apprehension in her daughter's demeanor. "This'll be great. We'll get to see Grandma and Grandpa every day."

Just as they'd planned. "Are you sure?" Sun asked, unconvinced.

She turned back and gestured to herself. "Mom, real clothes."

"Okay."

"I swear, I'm never wearing blue sweaters again."

Sun laughed softly and shrugged into her own jacket.

"Or plaid."

"Plaid?" Sun gasped. "You love plaid."

"Correction." After Auri scooped up her backpack, she held up an index finger to iterate her point. "I *loved* plaid. I found it adorable. Like squirrels. Or miniature cupcakes."

"Oh yeah. Those are great."

"But the minute plaid's forced upon you every day? Way less adorable."

"Gotcha."

"Okay," Auri said, facing her mother to give her a once-over. "Do you have everything?"

Sun frowned. "I think so."

"Keys?"

Sun patted her pants pocket. "Check."

"Badge?"

She tapped the shiny trinket over her heart. "Check."

"Gun?"

She scraped a palm over her duty weapon. "Check."

"Sanity?"

Sun's lids rounded. She whirled around, searching the area for her soundness of mind. She only had the one thread left. She couldn't afford to lose it. "Damn. Where did I have it last?"

"Did you look under the sofa?"

Keeping up the game, Sun dropped to her knees and searched under the sofa.

Auri shook her head, tsking as she headed for the side door. "I swear, Mom. You'd lose your head if that nice Dr. Frankenstein hadn't bolted it onto your body."

Sun straightened. "Did you just call me a monster?"

When her daughter only giggled, she hopped up and followed her out. They stepped onto the porch, and Sun breathed in the smell of pine and fresh snow and burning wood from fireplaces all over town.

Auri took a moment to do the same. She drew in a deep breath and turned back. "I think I love it here, Mom."

The affirmation in Auri's voice eased some of the tension twisting Sun's stomach into knots. Not all of it, but she'd take what she could get. "I do, too, sweetheart."

Maybe it was all in her imagination, but Auri hadn't seemed the same since she'd let her go to the supersecret New Year's Eve gathering at the lake. The annual party parents and cops weren't supposed to know about. The same parents and cops who began the tradition decades ago.

She'd only let Auri stay for a couple of hours. Could something have happened there? Auri hadn't been the same since that night, and Sun knew what could happen when teens gathered. The atmosphere could change from crazy-fun to multiple-stab-wounds in a heartbeat.

"You know, you can stay home a few more days. Your asthma has been kicking up, hon. And your voice is a little raspy. And—"

"It's okay. I don't want to get behind," she said.

"Do you have your inhaler?"

Auri reached into her coat pocket and pulled out the L-shaped contraption. "Yep."

A woman called out to them then. A feisty woman with graying blond hair and an inhuman capacity for resilience. "Tallyho!"

They turned as Elaine Freyr lumbered through the snow toward them, followed by her very own partner in crime, a.k.a. her roughish husband of thirty-five years, Cyrus Freyr.

Sun leaned closer to Auri. "Did your grandmother just call me a ho?"

"Hey, Grandma. Hey, Grandpa," Auri said, ignoring her.

It happened.

The girl angling for the Granddaughter of the Year award hurried toward the couple for a hug. "Mom's worried you guys are going to prison."

Elaine laughed and pulled the stool pigeon into her arms.

"Snitches get stitches!" Sun called out to her.

"Your mother's been saying that for years," Elaine said over Auri's shoulder, "and we haven't been to the big house yet." She let her go so Auri could give her grandfather the same treatment.

"Hi, Grandpa."

Cyrus took his turn and folded his granddaughter into his arms. "Hey, peanut. What are we going to prison for this time?"

Auri pulled back. "Election tampering."

"Ah. Should've known." Cyrus indicated the apartment with a nod. "What do you think of her?"

"She's beautiful, Grandpa."

His face glowed with appreciation as he looked at Sun. "And it's better than paying fifteen hundred a month for a renovated garage, eh?"

He had a point. Santa Fe was nothing if not pricey. "You got me there, Dad." She gave them both a quick hug, then headed toward her cruiser, the black one with the word sheriff written in gold letters across the side.

"Sunny, wait," her mother said, fumbling in her coat pocket. "We have to take a picture. It's Auri's first day of school."

Sun groaned out loud for her mother's benefit, hiding the fact that she found the woman all kinds of adorable. She was still angry with them. Or trying to be. They'd entered her into the election for sheriff without her consent. And she'd won. It boggled the mind.

"We're going to be late, Mom."

"Nonsense." She took out her phone and looked for the camera app. For, like, twenty minutes.

"Here." Sun snatched the phone away, fighting a grin. It would only encourage her. She swiped to the home screen, clicked on the app, and held the phone up for a selfie. "Come in, everyone."

"Oh!" Elaine said, ecstatic. She wrapped an arm into her husband's. "Get closer, hon."

The cold air had brightened all their faces. Sun snapped several shots of the pink-cheeked foursome, then herded her daughter toward the cruiser, her father quick on her heels.

When Auri went around to the passenger's side, Sun turned to face him.

He offered her a knowing smile and asked, "You okay? With all of this?"

She put a hand on his arm. "I'm okay, Dad. It's all good." *She hoped.* "But don't think for a second you're off the hook."

"I rarely am. It's just, I know how much you enjoyed putting this place in your rearview."

"I was seventeen. And one shade of nail polish away from becoming goth." She thought back. "Nobody needed to see that." After sliding him a cheeky grin, she stomped through the snow to the driver's side.

He cleared his throat and followed again, apparently not finished with the conversation. "Well, good. Good," he hedged before asking, "And how are you sleeping? Any, you know, nightmares?"

Ah. That's what this was about. Sun turned back and offered him her most reassuring smile. "No nightmares, Dad."

He nodded and opened the door as Elaine called out, "You and Auri have a good day. And don't forget about the meeting!"

Sun looked over the hood of her SUV. "What meeting?"

Elaine sucked in a sharp breath. "Sunshine Blaze Vicram."

She hopped inside the cruiser before her mother could get any further with that sentiment. Nothing good ever came after the words *Sunshine Blaze Vicram.*

She gave her eagle-eyed father one last smile of reassurance as he closed the door, then backed out of the snow-covered drive, confident she'd done the right thing. Telling him the truth would only exacerbate the guilt she could see gnawing at him every time he looked at her. There was no need for both of them to lose sleep over something that happened in Del Sol so very long ago.

AFTERWORD

Thank you for reading **A LOVELY DROP: A STORY OF THE NEVERNEATH**. We hope you enjoyed it! If you liked this book – or any of Darynda's other releases – please consider rating the book at the online retailer of your choice. Your ratings and reviews help other readers find new favorites, and of course there is no better or more appreciated support for an author than word of mouth recommendations from happy readers. Thanks again for your interest in Darynda's books!

Darynda Jones

www.daryndajones.com

Never miss a new book
From Darynda Jones!

Sign up for Darynda's newsletter!

Be the first to get notified of new releases and be eligible

for special subscribers-only exclusive content and giveaways.
Sign up today!

Also from DARYNDA JONES
(click to purchase)

PARANORMAL

BETWIXT & BETWEEN
Betwixt
Bewitched
Beguiled

CHARLEY DAVIDSON SERIES
First Grave on the Right
For I have Sinned: A Charley Short Story
Second Grave on the Left
Third Grave Dead Ahead
Fourth Grave Beneath my Feet
Fifth Grave Past the Light
Sixth Grave on the Edge
Seventh Grave and No Body
Eight Grave After Dark
Brighter than the Sun: A Reyes Novella
The Dirt on Ninth Grave
The Curse of Tenth Grave
Eleventh Grave in Moonlight
The Trouble with Twelfth Grave
Summoned to Thirteenth Grave
The Graveyard Shift: A Charley Novella

THE NEVERNEATH
A Lovely Drop
The Monster
Dust Devils: A Short Story of The NeverNeath

MYSTERY

SUNSHINE VICRAM SERIES
A Bad Day for Sunshine
A Good Day for Chardonnay
A Hard Day for a Hangover

YOUNG ADULT

Darklight Series
Death and the Girl Next Door
Death, Doom, and Detention
Death and the Girl he Loves

SHORT STORIES

Nancy: Dark Screams Volume Three
Sentry: Heroes of Phenomena: audiomachine
Apprentice
More Short Stories!

ACKNOWLEDGMENTS

I would like to thank my incredible editors, copyeditors, proofreaders, and intrepid mushers for this project, Theresa Rogers, Trayce Layne, and Casey Harris-Parks. Seriously, you guys rock so hard. I know when you put the words "blah, blah, blah" in the margins, something has gone terribly awry. Thank you for your guidance and encouragement.

As always, thank you to my warrior agent, Alexandra Machinist, who puts up with so much. So, so much.

And I'd love to thank my superhero executive assistant and cover designer for this work, Dana Alma. Your skills astound and humble me. And thank you to my wunnerful, honey bunny of a personal assistant who moonlights as my sister, Netters. Without the two of you, I am an empty, gelatin-like substance that scares children. Just thank you.

ABOUT THE AUTHOR

New York Times and *USA Today* Bestselling Author Darynda Jones has won numerous awards for her work, including a prestigious RITA®, a Golden Heart®, and a Daphne du Maurier, and her books have been translated into17 languages. As a born storyteller, she grew up spinning tales of dashing damsels and heroes in distress for any unfortunate soul who happened by. Darynda lives in the Land of Enchantment, also known as New Mexico, with her husband and two beautiful sons, the Mighty, Mighty Jones Boys.

CONNECT WITH DARYNDA ONLINE:

www.DaryndaJones.com
Facebook
Instragram
Goodreads
Twitter

Made in the USA
Monee, IL
25 June 2023

37118602R10073